THE
WARLORD

USA TODAY BESTSELLING AUTHOR
KALLY ASH

The Warlord
(Mac Tíre Mafia #1)

Copyright © 2022 by Kally ash
www.kallyash.com

Cover design by Sly Fox Cover Design
Interior design by Sly Fox Cover Design
Edited by Swish Design & Editing
Proofread by Swish Design & Editing

For you know who...

PROLOGUE

GRAYSON

NINE YEARS AGO...

I WAS DYING.

Especially if that sharp stabbing pain in my chest was anything to go by. As I waited for my final breath, I played around with the words in my mind, reorganizing them, although fuck knew why.

Dying, I was.

Was I dying?

I either sounded like a fucking Irish Yoda, or I was asking a question I already knew the answer to.

Then another thought hit me. *I was too young to die*, but when I lived the life I did, it wasn't unexpected.

Rolling my head to the side, I saw the still body of Kellan Quinn, his features unrecognizable on account of the rifle shell that had blown his face off. As soon as the shot hit its target, I knew it had been from a sniper. How else could they have gotten close enough to the most powerful man in Galway?

I sucked in a gasp, trying to feed some oxygen into my body, my chest feeling as if it was on fire. When a young man's face took up my field of vision, I blinked.

It was Finnan Quinn, Kellan's only son and now the leader of the Mac Tíre Clan. He shoved something onto the left side of my chest, making the air I was desperate to keep inside my lungs leak out as I groaned in pain. His mouth was moving—he was telling me something—but I couldn't hear him properly. Somehow, I knew it was important. Concentrating, I focused.

"...owe you, Kent. You saved my fucking life." He licked his lips. "I fucking owe you one in return."

Breathing became even harder then, and my eyelids shuttered closed.

I'd never given much thought to what dying would be like...

It turned out it was peaceful.

I

GRAYSON

STOP LOOKING AT HER GODDAMN FUCKING ASS,
you *goddamn pervert.*

I forced my gaze away from what was in front of me to
what was outside the small, rectangular window opposite
me instead. White fluffy clouds looked pillow-soft below,
a bright blue sky blazed overhead. I knew that once we
were below the cloud cover, shit was going to get dreary.
How could it not when you lived in one of the most
changeable climates in the world.

I'd been Stateside for the last five days, collecting
something that was owed to my boss—Finnan Quinn.

And that possession he now owned?

The only daughter of America's Irish mafia boss.

Sloane Kavanaugh.

The arrangement had been to 'purchase' her in an
auction. My job was to be the only bidder. Finnan had

been assured of that, but shit had gone sideways on the night.

Another man had bid over the agreed price, and I had very strict instructions on how much to spend. Once that limit had been reached, I was forced to withdraw, but I knew that wouldn't be the end of it. I knew I would get what I'd come for, even if I had to do a little B&E to achieve it.

Now, Sloane was lying with her head in my lap, wearing the oversized t-shirt she'd worn as pajamas on the night I'd abducted her. I took her from the apartment soundlessly, without having to kill the man who had outbid me or the woman he was with.

When I'd arrived at the airport and boarded the plane, I'd laid her out on the long bench seat, but ten minutes after we were in the air, she'd started crying out in her ketamine-fueled sleep, only settling when I touched her. Once she'd quieted, I tried to move away, but that seemed to agitate her more.

Which was how she'd ended up with her head on my lap. My legs were fucking numb from sitting in the same position for the last seven hours, having only disturbed her twice to go to the bathroom.

I glanced down when she let out a breathy sigh and rolled over, snuggling in more closely to my body, her face settling perilously near my crotch. The hem of her shirt rode up with her movement, flashing the curve of her ass barely covered by a scrap of black satin.

I shook my head and hissed a "fuck" out from between my clenched teeth.

The heat of her breath seemed to permeate through the crotch of my slacks, turning my dick to steel beneath the zipper. Sloane made a happy little chuffing sound and nuzzled even closer.

Jesus-fucking-Christ.

I tried to slide her back down my thighs, but the shift made her platinum blonde hair fall over my legs like a satin sheet. It looked so fucking soft. Reaching down, I ran the back of a finger along the silky length, then pulled back like I'd been burned. Bunching my hand into a fist, I placed it back onto the armrest and tried to slow my breathing.

"We're around forty minutes out, Mr. Kent."

My gaze gravitated to the stewardess who was working the flight, and I gave her a nod. "Thanks, Eline."

"Can I get you anything? Anything at all?"

Lust shimmered in her eyes. Eline was one of the regular stewardesses who worked the charters, and forty minutes was more than enough time to provide me with the special *service* she had in mind. She drew her hand to her collarbone and swept it down her chest to part her crisp white shirt. I caught a flash of her breasts and the lace bra that held them in check.

But I didn't feel like getting my dick sucked by her.

Don't get me wrong. She gave fan-fucking-tastic blow jobs, but as I grazed my fingers through Sloane's hair on my thigh, I realized I didn't want her lips wrapped around my dick right now.

"I'm fine. Thanks, Eline."

Eline's clear blue eyes drifted to the sleeping Sloane, then back to me. Plastering a plastic smile onto her lips, she said brightly, "No problem. I'll let you know when to buckle up in preparation for descent."

She sashayed off, swinging her ass in her sky-high heels and navy-blue pencil skirt. I waited for the regret to hit me, but it was curiously absent. My gaze shifted back down to Sloane, and I willed her to open her eyes.

I'd memorized their color.

They were the gray of a winter morning when the fog was rolling in off the hills, and you couldn't see your damn hand in front of your face. When every time you breathed in, it felt like your lungs were seizing.

Fuck, I couldn't be thinking about this.

Our clan had only a few rules…

Never rat out a member.

Don't talk to the police.

And never get involved with another member's girlfriend or wife.

The first two rules I was okay with. Once you were part of the clan, you were part of the clan for life. The only way out was in a pine box. And it would be a cold day in hell when I spoke to the cops about anything.

I stared at the woman with her head in my lap. Sloane belonged to my boss now, which meant that all these urges to touch her, I had to put a fucking stop to. Tell that to my fucking dick, though. It had been hard since the first time I saw her all those months ago.

Above my head, the seatbelt light illuminated, and I rearranged Sloane carefully to buckle myself in. A moment later, Eline came back through the cabin.

"She'll need a belt as well, Mr. Kent," she told me,

gesturing to the unconscious Sloane. "And we'll be landing in twenty, sir." She excused herself, leaving me to manhandle Sloane into one of the seats.

I rose from the chair, carefully moving Sloane's head from my lap as I did. Putting my hands under her arms, I lifted, feeling how warm she was. The hem of the shirt slid up when I sat her in the chair, my hands grazing the back of Sloane's toned, tanned thighs and brushing against warm satin that I knew was covering her ass.

My dick twitched as if reminding me it knew what it wanted.

Gritting my teeth, I went to buckle her in only to realize she was sitting on the two ends of the belt. I was forced to squeeze a hand under her ass again and feel around for the nylon sashes that ended with the two metal buckles. When I'd moved them out of the way, I secured the belt around her slim waist and retreated to the opposite seat.

I felt the plane begin its descent, and my fingers started tapping against my knee while my eyes stayed glued to Sloane's slack face. Her head was resting against the plush chair back, her t-shirt still bunched up around her hips, so I caught a flash of her satin-draped pussy.

"Fuck," I muttered to myself, unclipping my seatbelt and straightening the fabric, so it covered her legs from hip to top of the knee. Sitting back in my seat, I turned my attention to the window and watched as the plane sliced through the clouds—the white peaks turning a dour gray and revealing a rain-filled sky and sodden green land beneath.

There really was no place like home.

It was another fifteen minutes before the wheels hit the

tarmac at Knock Airport. Although mid-afternoon, the sky was dark, and the rain rolling down the windows started to get heavier. The plane taxied for a few minutes before finally coming to a smooth stop.

Outside, I saw a car waiting, where one of the sentinels would drive us to Galway, about an hour away. The seatbelt sign turned off, and I unbuckled my belt. I stood and undid Sloane's belt, picking her up gently and holding her against my chest.

Eline was just finishing the checks when I approached the front cabin door.

"If you give me a moment, I'll walk you down, Mr. Kent," Eline told me. She opened the main hatch and lowered the airstairs. Shaking out an umbrella she'd taken from a stowage hatch, she opened it and stepped to one side.

I followed her out, only getting hit by a few spots of rain before Eline wielded the umbrella like the professional she was. With her arm outstretched, she kept Sloane and me covered until we got to the black Range Rover.

Torin O'Rourke already had the rear door open and I slid into the back seat, settling Sloane in beside me. Torin slammed the door, shutting out the noise of the rain and the sound of plane engines.

In the muffled cool of the car, I let myself stare at Sloane. She was slumped against my chest, and I lifted my arm to settle it across her narrow shoulders.

She made a soft, contented noise, turning her face and pressing it more closely to my chest. Then she exhaled heavily, her warm breath reaching through the fibers of my shirt. The driver's side door opened and Torin slid inside.

"Caolan is here," Torin said.

I frowned. *Why in the hell was Caolan at the airport?* Before I could ask, the passenger door opened, and the man in question slid inside the car, shaking the rain off his jacket.

Caolan Daly was the clan's Quartermaster. At only a few inches shorter than me but a few years older, he held the rank of sergeant for the clan, and headed the team of my enforcers. Technically, the bastard was my boss, but we'd been friends since we were kids, and our management style was anything but normal.

He shoved some of his wet brown hair from his eyes and shut the door. "This fucking weather."

"You say that like it's fucking news," I replied.

He grinned, then narrowed his eyes at Sloane. "Is this the lass that was promised to Finnan?"

"Aye. Sloane Kavanaugh in the flesh."

Caolan looked her over, his green eyes lingering on her legs and ass a little too long for my liking. "She's a pretty lass. Finnan fucking lucked out with this deal."

I chewed the inside of my cheek. "Yeah. What are you doing here again?"

His smile turned into a frown. "A delivery was supposed to be coming in tonight, but the airplane's hold was empty when I looked. The airport staff said they didn't see anything out of the ordinary. It was like someone stole our shit from right under our noses."

Shit. Finnan had been keeping me updated on the deals that were falling through while I was away. Whenever there was a chance to make some money, another clan beat us to it. I had no idea how they were doing it, but Finnan wasn't going to hold his dick and do nothing. We just had to figure out *how* the other clans were getting their intel. My gut told me there was a rat in our ranks.

"We need to put an end to this shite," Caolan said vehemently.

I nodded, being one hundred percent on board with that. "Are you riding back with us?"

The other man's eyes drifted down to Sloane once more, and my hand curled into a tight fist. Somehow, the thought of having to share a car with him while he eyed the girl like that just about made me want to commit murder.

Which was ridiculous.

Because the lass wasn't mine.

She belonged to my boss.

"No. I have my own car waiting." His gaze drifted back to Sloane, and he said, "I just wanted to see what all the fuss was about."

My shoulders loosened. I hadn't even realized they were tight. "I'll see you around, Caolan."

With a wicked grin, Caolan popped open the door and stepped back out in the rain.

As soon as the door slammed shut, I told Torin, "Go."

He went, sliding the car into gear and pulling off the tarmac and out of the airport like he'd stolen the damn thing. With my free hand, I gripped the *oh-shit* handle, and my arm around Sloane tightened. We went around a corner, making her body slide more tightly against mine, and I gritted my teeth.

Having more of her soft curves against my body. That was just what the fuck I needed.

"Ease off, gobshite," I bit out.

Torin did, but not before his dark eyes flickered to the rearview mirror to look at me.

"She's pretty," he said.

"Yeah, what of it?" I barked back. *Fuck*. I needed to put a lid on this territorial bullshit. I glanced down at Sloane, then forced myself to release a breath and added, "Just get us back to Galway in one fucking piece."

He smirked. "Yes, sir."

2
SLOANE

I BECAME AWARE OF MY SURROUNDINGS SLOWLY. At first, I wasn't sure anything had changed from the last time this had happened, but I let myself absorb the sensations. My face was pressed against something warm and slightly scratchy, but when I inhaled, I damn near moaned in pleasure. It smelled of sandalwood, leather, and pine.

Something hard and hot was banded around my shoulders, holding me close to the firm, muscled body I was lying on. There was a low-level growl of a high-powered engine. I knew it was an engine because my father had cars that sounded the same. Supercharged. Lots of torque.

We were moving, and until we'd slowed down to take a corner and I nearly rolled off whatever delicious thing I was laying on, I hadn't known just how fast.

Whoever was behind the wheel was driving like they'd stolen it, accelerating rapidly, braking late, and yanking on the wheel like they were over-correcting.

"Ease off, gobshite," someone said acidly with an Irish brogue that seemed to have the ability to melt my panties. The flat-out roar of the engine became a subdued purr.

"She's pretty," another voice said. *Male.* He also had an Irish accent, but this one didn't do it for me like the first man's.

"Yeah, what of it?" Another terse response and I wondered what had this guy's panties in a twist. "Just get us back to Galway in one fucking piece."

"Yes, sir."

I stayed still for a few moments more, intending to continue pretending I wasn't awake yet, when the man said softly and too close to my ear, "I know you're awake, lass."

I needed a little more time to figure out what I was going to do. I could keep pretending, or I could face the man who had abducted me from my estranged mother mere hours after reuniting with her.

I jerked into a sit, and he let me go, resettling one arm onto the top of his thigh while casually propping the other onto the passenger window sill. I would've enjoyed the view a little more if my stomach wasn't revolting at the same time.

The man staring back at me was tall with ice-blue eyes and dark blond hair. His jaw was chiseled and covered in careless stubble, his nose just slightly crooked like it had been broken and not reset perfectly straight. I swallowed, feeling my libido sit up and take notice even if the rest of my body was trying to escape out of my mouth.

My gaze dropped to look at the rest of him. Even though he was wearing black slacks and a white, open-collar business shirt, I suspected he was stacked with carefully built muscle. When I saw the tattoo of what looked like a dog created in Celtic whorls on his right hand, my tongue swiped across my bottom lip.

His arctic eyes dropped to my mouth and his jaw bulged. "How are you feeling?"

Doing a mental inventory of my body, I realized the nauseous feeling I'd experienced when I'd woken up was only getting worse. "Like I'm going to be sick."

He leaned forward, reaching into the pouch at the back of the chair in front. He retrieved a plastic vomit bag, like what you get at the hospital, and pulled out the bag from the hard inner plastic ring. Handing it to me wordlessly, he sat back in his chair and watched me.

I studied the tattoo on his hand while holding the ring that served as the mouthpiece. It smelled of cheap plastic and the leather from the chair. I wondered whether the leather I'd smelled before was from the upholstery or whether it belonged to the man beside me.

"Do you remember who I am?" he finally asked after studying me for longer than socially acceptable.

Did I? I racked my brain, trying to work through what had happened. I'd met my mom and her partner, Dagger. He'd gone all Neanderthal on her and dragged her to bed. I'd gone to bed too, changing into an oversized t-shirt— glancing down, I saw I was still wearing it.

I narrowed my eyes at him. "You better not have taken any liberties with me."

He cocked an arrogant brow. "Liberties, lass? What kind of liberties?"

"The kind where I was unconscious and in little more than a shirt and panties. Those kinds of liberties."

He turned away and looked out the window, but I noticed the hand on his thigh flexing into a tight fist. My eyes went back to his face when he said, "No. No liberties. You aren't mine."

I bristled. "I don't belong to anyone."

He turned back—his blue eyes resigned. "That's where you're wrong, lass." He scrubbed a hand through his hair. "Why aren't you hysterical right now?"

"What good would hysterics do me?" I replied, arching a brow. The look would've been much more dramatic if I didn't have my face in the top of a vomit bag, but my stomach was still roiling, and bile was a bitter bite in the back of my throat.

"You were kidnapped."

"I'm aware."

"And taken to another country."

I peered out the window, staring at the lush green fields and low stone walls that zoomed past the glass. The sky was gray, the clouds heavy and full with more rain to come. I sure wasn't in Detroit anymore. The problem was, I hadn't even been out of the state before, so I had no idea what other areas of the country looked like. Somehow, I didn't think they looked like this.

"Where are we?" I didn't turn to face him, not wanting him to see the flicker of unease that was building inside my chest.

"Ireland. About forty minutes north of Galway, to be precise."

I swallowed over the hard lump in my throat and turned to face the man who had abducted me. "Who are you?"

"Grayson Kent."

Blinking rapidly, I willed my brain to focus on the memory. I remembered waking up in an airplane and a man—*Grayson*—telling me not to scream, but my father had taken me through enough abduction drills to know if someone tells you not to scream, that you should do just the opposite. If your kidnapper wanted you quiet, it meant they were in a public place where drawing attention to them would be bad.

I had screamed, and although he'd given me the chance to be a good and obedient little abductee, I hadn't wanted to give him the satisfaction. He'd shoved his hand over my mouth and stuck me with a needle.

He had told me then that his name was Grayson, right before I'd drifted into the drug haze.

"Who's your boss?" My question came out quietly—so quietly I wasn't sure he'd heard me.

I tried again. "Grayson, who—"

"Finnan Quinn." He turned to face me—his expression unreadable. "The man who's going to be your husband in two weeks."

Finnan Quinn.

Finnan Quinn.

Finnan Quinn.

I repeated the name to myself, shuffling through my mental inventory—the same inventory my father had made me memorize. Allies. Enemies. Major players. All of them. Finnan Quinn was the boss of the Mac Tíre Clan—one of Ireland's more ruthless mafia groups.

My grandfather had previously had dealings with them, but not my father.

I licked my suddenly dry lips and Grayson's blue eyes darkened as he watched the movement. "Finnan Quinn is to be my husband?"

"Aye."

"In two weeks?"

Grayson's expression went blank. "Aye."

"Why?"

"That's something you'll have to discuss with him, lass."

I didn't understand why, but the way he said *lass* to me, made something flutter in my chest.

Which was bad.

Stockholm Syndrome wasn't an option.

"Are you taking me to him now?"

"Soon. He wants to meet you. Make sure you're safe."

"I didn't think he'd care either way for my mental and physical welfare considering the current situation."

Grayson cocked his head to one side. "And what situation is that?"

"He abducted me. Or should I say he had *you* abduct me and taken to another country."

"You were abducted, I admit that, but you belonged to him first. You were promised to him, lass."

I narrowed my eyes and pressed myself more snuggly against the rear door. "Promised? How? Why?"

He shook his head. "These are all questions you can ask

him. We'll be there in forty minutes."

"I…" *Fuck.* That bile that had only been threatening the back of my throat was now making a full-blown run for the exit. A small, strangled sound escaped me, and Grayson sat up in alarm.

He reached for me but stopped short of touching. "Lass?"

"I'm going to be—" I didn't get to finish my sentence. The nausea that had been sitting in the background during our tête-à-tête decided it'd had enough. It bubbled up from my stomach and burned my throat. Bending my head, squeezing shut my eyes, I vomited the meager contents of my stomach into the plastic bag, hating every damn second of it. Vomiting was bad. Vomiting in front of an audience was worse. Puking in front of a man as good-looking as Grayson was a damn crying shame.

I was mortified when he brushed my loose hair back from my face, gathering the long length into his big fist. I had a momentary thought of him doing that to me while I was naked and on my knees, but lusting after the man who kidnapped me was bad. I'd already established that fact.

I wanted the earth to open up and swallow me whole when he started murmuring softly to me in that lilting accent of his, telling me things like *it was going to be okay, it would be over soon,* and *they could pull over to wash my face and get me something to drink.*

The car slowed, then turned, before finally coming to a complete stop. I had a quick glance out the window to see we'd pulled into a gas station called Applegreen. It was a big building with the forecourt leading into what looked like a convenience store with a restaurant off to one side. It was early afternoon according to the clock in the car, but with the rain cover, it was dark, so the bright lights were on—green and white fluorescents shining the way across the rain-soaked pavement.

Grayson touched my chin, and I slanted him with a look. He held up what looked like an honest-to-God handkerchief. "Just trying to clean off your chin."

When I said nothing, he reached forward, wiping away some vomit that hadn't made it into the bag. The gesture was strangely intimate, and I pulled away, staring at him.

"You have five minutes to get cleaned up," he rasped. "Torin, go with her. Make sure she doesn't do something stupid."

"Aye, boss," the driver—Torin—replied and got out. He slammed the door shut, and it was just Grayson and me.

I crossed my arms over my chest. "I'm not going with him."

"Take that puss off your face. You *are* going with him. You wanted to get cleaned up. Get cleaned up. We don't have time for this shite. And don't even think about legging it."

"*Legging it? Take that puss off my face?* What the hell does that mean?"

"Run away and don't sulk," he begrudgingly replied. "Don't do anything stupid. Torin is bigger than you, as well as armed."

I wasn't intimidated. "And if I did *leg it*? What then, huh?"

He pushed his face close to mine, and I automatically pulled back. I smelled of vomit and the idea that he was smelling it on my breath embarrassed me.

Unaware of my personal dilemma, he growled, "Then I would chase you down, *lass*, and when I caught you, you would not like what would happen next."

An unbidden shiver tracked down my spine at the thought of what Grayson could do to me. I hoped it was something that involved very few clothes and a spanking for being such a bad girl. I shook my head, and he must've taken that as my acquiescence because he eased back in his seat.

I yelped when Torin opened the door I was leaning on, and I nearly tumbled out. It was only Grayson's hand on my arm that stopped me from toppling back, but it was enough physical contact to let me feel the spark that arced between us.

When he was sure I wasn't going to go backward out of the car, he said gruffly, "Get cleaned up."

"Won't people stare at me? I'm not exactly dressed."

Glaring, he said, "Get cleaned up. Everybody knows who Torin is around here."

Left with the cryptic statement hovering in the air, I let Torin help me from the car and lead the way through the forecourt. There were a few other motorists around, but none of them paid attention to me, which was surprising given how incredibly underdressed I was.

How much power did the Mac Tíre Clan have around here?

If they were anything like my father, it would've been a lot.

A cold wind whipped through the air, sending a rush of

goose bumps teeming up my arms and legs. Wrapping my arms around my middle, I hustled to keep up with Torin as we stepped into the convenience store.

The lights were harsh, and I blinked at the glare. There were dark gray tiles on the floor, all running away from the door as if leading you in by the eye. Low and mid-level shelving took up more of the floor space, except for a large open area in front of the cashiers, who stood behind a slightly raised desk stuffed with candy, gum, and chips. The brightly-colored bags of snacks looked appealing and that was when I knew I wasn't feeling well.

"The bathroom is through there." Torin's words drew me from my surveillance.

"What?"

He pointed to an alcove beside an ATM. "The bathroom. Get washed up. I'll get some water."

Oh, the restroom. "Can I get some chips too? Maybe some chocolate?"

His mouth quirked up in a smile. "Sure. Anything else?"

I shook my head and padded—barefoot—toward the restroom. There weren't separate male and female toilets. Rather there was only one door with a sign on the front that featured a man and a woman side-by-side but separated by a line. I glanced down at the lock and saw that the writing was green, so I pushed inside.

More of that same dark gray tile covered the floor. There were patches that were damp, and I looked down at my feet again. They were going to get covered in whatever-the-fuck was on the floor, but like I had a choice.

Until I saw a paper towel dispenser on the wall.

I prayed to the restroom gods that there were some left. Tiptoeing and using as little of my feet as possible, I made my way across the small space and drew out a handful of the paper towel before scattering it onto the tile. When I had it sufficiently covered, I hovered over the toilet seat and emptied my bladder. After, I washed my hands, then started working on cleaning the vomit from my face.

Some had gotten into my hair even though Grayson had done his best to hold it back, but like I was going to bitch about that. It could've been a whole lot worse. I did what I could to wash it out, and was just holding it under the hand dryer when someone banged on the door.

"*Occupado*," I called out, finger combing my hair.

The knocking got louder.

"I'm busy!" I yelled over the hand dryer, hoping whoever was out there would leave. It was probably Torin. It had been a lot longer than five minutes, and Grayson must've been climbing up his ass for it. I didn't know why, but that made me smile.

The hammering started again, and I heaved a sigh.

"Lass, let me in."

It was Grayson.

My lady parts started to throb, but I shut my eyes and tried to ignore it. My body was messed up from the drugs. That's why it was reacting the way it was.

"Lass?" he called again, this time his voice lowering a few octaves. "Sloane, let me in this minute, or I'll bust my way in."

Walking to the door, I flipped the lock, then quickly stepped back. As expected, Grayson's anger boiled into the room before he did, giving me a minute to prepare to meet his ire.

"I'm not finished." I gestured to my damp hair.

His blue gaze flickered from my face, down my body, then to the floor where I was standing on my tip-toes to avoid the now damp paper towel nest. "What the fuck have you done in here?"

"I made it clean enough for me to walk on. In case you haven't noticed, I don't have any shoes, and who the hell knows what's been on this floor."

His jaw bulged right before he grabbed my arm and jerked me toward him. I was pressed against his body for a moment, his sandalwood and leather scent drowning out the smell of fake lemon soap and urine, then I was swung up into his arms.

"Put me down!"

"No. You want to be precious about what you're fucking putting your feet on? How about you don't put them anywhere."

"Put me down this instant!"

Ignoring me, he walked out into the convenience store, where I expected people to gawk. Every person in there barely looked our way, all going about their business paying for gas or getting snacks. Torin was waiting for us by the door, his face set into a smirk. I flipped him off as we stepped outside, then shivered when the wind blew hard against my legs and ass.

I started to struggle in Grayson's arms.

"Keep still, or I'll drop you."

"Everyone can see my ass right now," I said softly.

He hesitated a step, then grumbled something under his breath. Bringing his big hand under the shirt, his warm palm covered me from the tops of my thighs to the small of my back. Knowing that he was essentially cupping my pussy right now made heat rise to my cheeks.

When he got back to the Range Rover, he had to wait for Torin to open the rear door. Inside, he placed me on the seat, withdrawing his strong arms and warm hands from beneath me. For a moment, he simply stood there, staring at me from only a few inches away. It wasn't until Torin opened the driver's side door that the spell was broken. Grayson's eyes lingered for a moment longer before he shut my door and stalked around to the other side.

Drawing my legs up onto the seat, I wrapped my arms around them and rested my cheek on my knees.

"Buckle up," Grayson said gruffly after he closed his own door. Honestly, I didn't think the guy had any other mode but gruff. I did as he asked, though, bringing the nylon sash over my shoulder and sliding the silver latch plate into the buckle.

"Here are your Taytos, lass."

I glanced up to see Torin holding out a bright pink and blue bag to me.

"My what?"

"Taytos. Crisps." I must've looked puzzled because he said in a fake American accent, "Chips."

I reached for them, reading what flavor it said they were on the front. *Prawn cocktail*. That didn't sound the least bit appealing. But my stomach was unsettled, and having something both greasy and salty in it would make me feel better. I murmured a "thank you" and opened the packet. He bobbed his head and started the engine, leaving the gas station and getting us back onto the highway.

3

GRAYSON

MY HANDS FLEXED INTO FISTS BEFORE RELAXING, but no matter what I did, I could still feel her smooth skin. I could still feel the heat coming from her pussy. I hadn't meant to touch her there, but she was so small, and my hand was so big, and there was some inevitability about it all. She had stiffened in my arms ever so slightly, but that only made me want to hold her a little tighter—a little closer.

The sound of crunching snapped me from the visceral memories, and I glanced over to find Sloane chewing thoughtfully on her first real Irish crisp. She was looking out the window, so I stared at her profile, taking the time to enjoy it. Reaching down, she took another chip from the bag and popped it into her mouth.

"If you keep staring at me, I won't be able to eat," she said after a moment.

"I'm not staring," I replied automatically.

She looked at me, one platinum brow winging up. "Oh, you're not. I must've mistaken your eyes on me for something else then."

My jaw bulged and my cock jerked to attention. Resettling myself into my seat so that the damn thing wasn't so fucking obvious, I said, "You eat with your mouth open. It's very unbecoming for a young lady."

Her mouth popped open in surprise before she realized what she'd done and closed it again. "I do *not* eat with my mouth open."

I shrugged but said nothing more. When I glanced over, I found her frowning at me, her nostrils flaring delicately. She was gorgeous when she was pissed off. I turned away, but I could still see her reflection in my window. Her gaze had traveled down my body, but when her eyes had gotten to my hips, she bit her bottom lip and stared.

Fuck. She'd seen it.

"Now who's the one who's staring," I said quietly, hoping to shame her into looking away.

She cleared her throat and did just that, busying herself with the crisps once more.

My phone started to ring, and I pulled it from the pocket of my slacks. It was Finnan. Probably checking up on his future bride. Sliding my finger across the screen, I answered the call.

"Finnan, we're in the car."

"Torin told me you had to stop."

"Sloane wasn't well. She needed to clean up."

"How's she doing now?"

I glanced over at her. She was watching me, worrying at her bottom lip with her teeth. "Seems better."

"Good. I'll meet you when you get here."

I hung up, sliding the phone back into my pocket.

"Was that my *husband-to-be*?" she asked mockingly.

"Yes, it was. He's looking forward to meeting you."

"He couldn't get a woman to marry him without throwing abduction in as foreplay?"

I tried to hide my smile. The woman had a sass mouth—something I wasn't sure Finnan would like, but I sure as hell did. "He's got plenty of women to choose from, but he's not marrying for love. Or sex."

"What's he marrying for then?"

"Power."

She blinked her dove-gray eyes at me. "How is he going to gain power off marrying me?"

I scrutinized her face. She didn't seem the least bit concerned that she was being married off to a stranger.

"Why doesn't this bother you?"

"Define *this*? Getting sick then being forced to walk barefoot on a disgusting public restroom floor? Enjoying these damn prawn cocktail *crisps* so much?" She brandished the bag at me. "Or is it that I've been sold to a man like a piece of property?"

In the front, Torin cleared his throat like he was trying to disguise a laugh.

I ignored him and said, "The last one. The property one."

"My father taught me to always expect something like this to happen to me one day."

I couldn't help it. I arched a brow. "Arranged marriage?"

She rolled her eyes. "Abduction. By the time I was thirteen, there had been two attempted kidnappings and one attempt on my life. My father started going through abduction drills after that."

"What else did your father do?"

"Taught me how to shoot. How to use knives. Martial arts. Jujitsu. Kickboxing."

Damn, all of that was a fucking turn-on. I stroked my stubbled jaw.

"Since you won't tell me *how* this betrothal to Finnan came about, at least tell me a bit about him."

"He's a fair man but ruthless. If you cross him, expect the retribution to be swift and fatal. He doesn't share his things, so when you become his, I recommend you avoid staring at other men too long or engaging them in conversation. And for the love of all things holy, don't flirt with someone else."

In a sugary voice, she replied, "He sounds like a treat. Anything else I should know?"

"Yeah, he doesn't like smart mouths, so I suggest you keep yours in check while you're with him."

Her nostrils flared in anger, but instead of running her mouth again, she popped another crisp onto her tongue and chewed. Sloane stared out the window, and I realized she was giving me the silent treatment. Fuck, it felt like I was looking at my sister, Fallon, when she got pissy with me. Sloane may have only been eighteen, but her maturity level was far beyond those years—except for now, clearly.

Pulling out my phone, I dialed my sister's number.

She answered on the first ring. "Big brother! I was just thinking about you."

I narrowed my eyes and wiped some lint from the leg of my slacks. "Why doesn't that fill me with confidence?"

"I was just telling my girlfriend about you. She's single." She said that last part in a sing-song voice.

"No, Fallon."

"You can't say no yet. You don't even know a thing about her."

I scrubbed a hand over my face. "If she's your friend, that's all I need to know."

"Alana is lovely. Tall. Blonde hair. Blue eyes. All your favorites!"

"No."

"I've shown her your photo. She thinks you're cute."

"I don't know how many other ways I can say this, Fallon, but the answer is still no."

"You're no fun."

I could practically see the pout on her face. "What are you doing right now?"

"Alana and I are about to meet up with some friends from the course at the pub for dinner. Then we're hitting one of the clubs in town."

I was instantly on alert. "Is that such a good idea?"

"I'll be fine, Grayson. I've been doing well. No slips. No mishaps."

I ground my molars. "I think it's too soon."

She heaved a resigned sigh, then lowered her voice. "I need this, Gray. I haven't seen my friends in six months. I dropped off the fucking planet, but I'm good. I've been seeing the shrink. I've been going to meetings."

"What about Ava? What does she think?"

Yeah, throwing her therapist into the conversation was a dick move, but I had to be sure.

The acoustics of the call changed like she'd taken herself to a more private space to talk. "She thinks it's time."

"She thinks it's time to go to a pub, then a club? Now? At this juncture?"

Fallon was silent for a moment. I hoped to hell she was actually thinking this through. "I miss going out, Gray."

My eyes shuttered shut. Her tone of voice slayed me. When I opened them, I let out a deep breath and said, "Do you need me to come with you tonight? You know, to keep you accountable?"

"You would do that for me?"

"My boss will give me the time. Just say the word."

"Then that would be nice. Thank you."

"Okay. Text me the name of the club. I'll meet you there."

"Okay," she whispered. "Love you, Gray."

"Love you, Fallon," I replied gruffly. I hung up, then glanced up to see Sloane staring at me.

4

SLOANE

"WAS THAT YOUR GIRLFRIEND?" I ASKED STIFFLY, smoothing the t-shirt over my legs.

Grayson didn't answer me.

Instead, he sat forward in his chair and spoke to Torin in a language I didn't understand.

"What did you say to him?" I demanded when he sat back.

A smug smile flexed into existence on his face, and my ovaries started to applaud. "Nothing that concerns you, lass."

"What language were you speaking to one another?"

"Gaelic."

"You know it's rude to speak another language in front of a person who doesn't understand it."

His smile brightened. "I guess you'll have to rectify that then."

Glowering at him, I let that comment go and stared back out the window. It wasn't just a sea of endless black now. There were more lights flickering into existence, but they were still far away. It wasn't long before houses appeared sporadically then as we got closer to Galway, more industrial buildings appeared.

The rain had yet to stop, leaving the road and building roofs slick. Eventually, Torin drove into what I assumed was the center of the city. The buildings here looked commercial, with a few stores and restaurants dotted throughout. He turned onto a street where buildings hugged one side, and a flood-lit harbor took up residence on the other.

Concrete bollards joined together with chunky, heavy, weather-worn chains kept the pedestrians walking along the harbor-side of the street from stepping out on the road. I wondered whether the air would smell of salt or whether the pervasive scent of fish had taken over.

As if reading my mind, Grayson wound down his window. Salt spray with an undertone of fishiness hit me in the face, but I breathed deep. I felt like I hadn't had fresh air in an age.

"You like the water?" Grayson asked, his rasping voice like some sort of audible caress in the darkness of the car.

I nodded. "My father has a house on Macatawa Bay back home."

"It's just your father's house? Not yours?"

"I never thought of it as mine. It's just a house. Never a home for me."

He gestured to what I assumed was Galway's harbor and asked, "It's like this?"

"No, but the smell is the same. Ever notice that?"

Grayson grunted and wound the window back up again. I cocked an eyebrow at him.

"Bulletproof glass isn't bulletproof if the window is open," he said by way of explanation.

Torin slowed the car, pulling into an underground parking lot. Concrete soared on all sides of the car as we descended the ramps until we finally pulled to a stop. Peering out the windshield, I saw we'd come to a security gate with thick vertical bars. Torin pulled down the driver's side visor and hit a button on a remote, and the door trundled open.

As we eased through the gate, I saw there were enough parking spaces for another ten cars. Torin pulled into the one closest to the elevator and shut off the engine.

I reached for the door latch but stopped when Grayson said, "Don't get out until Torin is outside your door."

"Why not?"

"If there's a shooter somewhere, you won't get hit if Torin is there."

I felt my eyes widen. "You expect him to take a bullet for me? I barely know the guy, and he barely knows me."

"It doesn't matter. He knows what his job is."

Glancing around the deserted garage, I asked, "Are you expecting shooters to be in here? I mean, we're in a secured parking area." There had been a better chance of getting shot when we'd stopped at that gas station.

"I've learned to expect shooters to be around every corner, lass."

Before I could ask him to explain, Torin opened my door, and I stepped out. The concrete was cold on my feet, but at least the surface was dry and relatively clean. Not knowing where to go, I stood there until Grayson rounded the rear of the car and stepped up beside me.

"What is this place?"

"You'll be staying here before the wedding. The apartment is secure. It's private, and you'll have guards with you around the clock."

I still wasn't sold on this idea of being a bride, but instead of bitching, I simply said, "Okay."

He led the way toward the elevator while Torin took up a position behind me. Grayson depressed the 'up' button, then slid his hand to the small of his back where a Glock was holstered. Shame on me for not noticing. He pulled the gun free and held it down against his thigh.

The elevator doors slid open smoothly, and I followed Grayson into the elevator. Torin stayed where he was, tipping an imaginary hat my way as the doors slid shut. We traveled to the top floor, and he stepped out first before waving me forward.

I followed—meekly—at his back as his long legs ate up the distance between the elevator and a door marked with the number eight. Pulling a key from his pocket, he unlocked the door and gestured for me to go inside.

"You don't want to check it first?" I asked.

"Two of my men were in here just before we got in the elevator. It's clear."

Sucking in a breath, I stepped into an apartment that could only be described as sterile. The walls were white, as were the carpets and furniture. Down a short hall, I emerged into a kitchen with white marble countertops and white upper and lower cabinets. I shivered.

"Are you cold?" Grayson asked, walking over to the thermostat on the wall. He fiddled with the knobs and buttons for a moment, and then I felt a blast of warm air coming from the vents above me.

"Thank you."

"Well, this is the kitchen… obviously. Living room. There are two bedrooms down the hall as well as a bathroom. Your bedroom also has an en suite." He walked to the fridge and pulled it open. The shelves were filled with food. "Everything you might need has been anticipated. You're safe here, Sloane."

Despite his reassurances, I wrapped my arms around myself. "So, what happens now?"

"Finnan will be here shortly—" He was interrupted by a phone call. Holding up a finger, he answered the call, turning his back on me. Whoever he was speaking to, after the initial *hello*, they spoke in Gaelic. When he hung up, Grayson turned to face me.

"That was Finnan. He can't make it to see you tonight. He sends his apologies, but he's going to reschedule dinner to tomorrow night."

"I don't have the option to say *no*, do I?" I asked.

Grayson shook his head like he regretted his answer. "No, lass."

I shrugged. "Okay. Fine. Tomorrow night. What about right now? And tonight? You don't expect me to stay put, do you?"

A muscle feathered in his jaw. "Finnan told me to take care of you tonight, so you'll be coming out with me later."

I arched a brow. "Take care of me? You said he was a possessive bastard. Why would he entrust me with you?"

"Because that's my job."

"Where are we going tonight?"

Ignoring my question, he said, "I'll be back to pick you up later. There are guards outside and on every level of this apartment building. Don't do something stupid."

Thumbing at my chest, I said, "*Moi?* Do something stupid?"

With a growl, he turned and left, locking the door behind him.

5

GRAYSON

RUNNING A HAND THROUGH MY HAIR, I CURSED that woman again. Cursed her for pushing me for information, and I cursed myself for giving it to her so easily. Lying to her about Finnan's whereabouts had caused a kick in my stomach. He couldn't meet her because he'd been getting his dick sucked by one of the girls at Velvet—the strip club the clan owned and operated.

He wasn't even married yet, and he was already fucking around. Finnan didn't have a goddamn clue what kind of woman had landed in his lap. Downstairs, I got back into the Rover.

"Where to?" Torin asked.

"Velvet."

He drove us out of the garage, then across town to the club. Parking out back, I got out and walked straight to the steel door. It opened before I could get there, one of our men holding it. Mack Nolan was the epitome of what it meant to be Irish. Flame-red hair, which he often kept hidden under a cap. Pale skin. Freckles. He was a fucking inferno waiting to go up if the sun ever got to him.

"Where is he?" I asked.

"In one of the private rooms with Delux."

I ground my teeth and stepped into the club's backstage area. The erotic pulse of music hit my already inflamed libido, and I braced for the onslaught of nearly naked women. I was so fucking wound up that I knew I needed to take the edge off. Instead of going into the club, I wandered into the dressing room, where I found at least a dozen of our girls either in the process of getting ready or cooling off after doing their set.

One of the girls—Rhapsody—squealed when she saw me, leaping from her seat and throwing herself at me. Her blonde hair extensions smacked me in the face as I stood there and absorbed the feeling of her hot, slightly sweaty body against mine.

"You come to see me, daddy?" she asked, finger-walking her way up my chest.

The truth was, any warm body would do. "Yeah, baby. Want to come and take my edge off?"

She reached down and took my hand, pulling me out of the dressing room and into one of the private offices at the rear. Rhapsody shut the door, engaged the lock, then sashayed over to me, where I leaned on the edge of the desk. Her blue eyes roved my face, down my chest, and to the bulge in the front of my slacks. She didn't need to know that the hard-on I was currently not trying to hide was all because of a sass-mouthed American I had no right to lust after.

Dropping her to her knees, she undid my belt buckle and button on my slacks with practiced hands. Once the zipper was down, she reached her greedy hand inside and stroked my cock through the thin fabric of my black boxer briefs. It kicked against her palm, and the look she gave me was downright sinful.

Leaning forward, she tongued at my dick through the material, wetting it with her wicked tongue and hot breaths. "Want me to suck this, daddy?"

What I really wanted was for her to stop damn talking.

Dipping my chin, I unclenched my jaw and said, "Take it to the back of your throat and choke on it."

And she did.

Gleefully.

Rhapsody took my whole length, her lack of a gag reflex meaning I could literally fuck her tonsils, and her throat never convulsed. She moved up and down me, touching herself as she worked, making these ridiculous porn moans down low in her throat. Fisting her hair, I pulled—getting an unwelcome flash of when I'd held Sloane's hair back as she'd vomited.

Fuck, don't think about her now.

But it was too late.

Rhapsody had become Sloane in my fucked-up head. It was her pretty mouth around my dick. Her platinum hair sliding over my knees and pooling in my lap. They were her moans of pleasure, although they didn't sound like bad porn now. They sounded wanton—desperate—like what she needed more than her next breath was for me to come down the back of her throat.

"Fuck!" My balls drew up and tightened, and with thoughts of Sloane dancing through my dick, I came. I came so hard I thought I stopped breathing for a moment—for a lifetime—as Sloane sucked me down, draining every last drop from my body.

When I finally came back to myself, I blinked down at the yellow-blonde head bobbing on my dick, and reality hit me like a hammer to the back of my skull. This wasn't Sloane, and I was fucking messed up to be thinking about her while getting my dick sucked by another woman.

"Enough," I growled, pushing her away and tucking my now completely limp dick back into my slacks. I leveraged myself upright, then took Rhapsody's face in my hand, turning it to the side so I could kiss her cheek. "Thanks, baby. That feels better."

Her blue eyes were fixed on my face as she ran a finger over her bottom lip, making sure her lipstick hadn't been ruined. "My pleasure," she purred.

I turned to leave but stopped when she called out, "When can you return the favor?"

Staring at her over my shoulder, I watched her run her hands over her breasts and dip down between her legs. Her whole body writhed.

"Maybe later, baby." I turned and walked to the end of the hall, pushing out of the staff corridor and backstage area and into the club. I scanned the dimly lit space, looking for Finnan, wondering whether he'd be done with Delux yet. When it was clear he hadn't emerged from whatever private room he was using, I strolled to the bar, where Mary Healy, our clan's Pull, was working.

Mary was in her sixties and had the look of a strict schoolmarm who didn't take any shit. Being the mother of eight head-strong daughters, she was adept at handling disputes among clan members. Aside from covering the bartender when she went on breaks, Mary was also the club's Mother—the woman who kept all the girls emotional and sexual health in check.

"Get you a drink, Grayson?" she asked, already placing a squat glass down onto the polished surface and palming the bottle of whisky. When she began to pour, I motioned for her to keep going with a circular motion with my fingers, then tapped when it was half full. "Rough day?"

I picked up the glass and knocked back the whole thing.

Mary filled it again.

"I guess you could say that."

"Want to talk about it?"

"Not really."

"Hey, Mary, can I get two double whiskies, please? Oh, hey, Grayson."

I turned to look at Kitty, one of the veterans of Velvet, even though she was barely twenty-five. She was dressed in purple tonight—her garter, bra, and panties all matching.

"How are you doing, Kitty?"

She hiked a hand onto her hip and grinned. "Good tippers in tonight, so maybe I'll be able to get Celeste into those ballet classes she wants to go to."

"How old is she now?" I asked.

"Five going on fifteen," she replied with a fond smile, nodding to Mary as she placed the drink order onto her waiting tray. Kitty picked it up without so much as losing a drop of liquor and waved goodbye.

"Her ex is sniffing around again," Mary said beside me, and I turned to look at her.

"He is?"

"Comes in the nights she's not working, asking the other girls questions about whether she's seeing anyone."

Motherfucker. "You need me to handle it?"

The older woman shook her head and patted my hand in that grandmotherly way she had. "I didn't tell you so you could give your bullets a new home. I told you, so you were aware. Finnan has lost interest in the day-to-day of this place. He only seems to want to reap the benefits. Someone needs to know what's going on beyond the profit margin."

"Thanks, Mary. I'll speak to the bouncers about not letting him in anymore."

Throwing back the rest of my drink, I settled the glass onto the bar and went in search of Little John. I found the bastard at the front door, his meaty fists clasped in front of his groin, his dark eyes narrowing on a group of lads stumbling through the door. His bald head nearly reached the ceiling—all seven-burly-feet of him filling the small entranceway.

He caught the eye of one of the men, his stare like an arctic blast. He didn't even have to say a word before the patron nodded and warned the rest of his buddies.

"Little John," I said.

He turned his head. "Kent."

"Have you seen Kitty's ex coming through in the last few weeks?"

He bobbed his head. "Sure. He's been around. Never when Kitty is on, though."

I clenched my jaw tight. "That stops today. We understood?"

"Aye. I'll let the others know. What do you want us to do with him when he comes?"

"Don't let him in, and if he wants to know why, tell him he can come speak to me."

Little John said, "Consider him banned."

Turning, I saw Shay O'Leary—looking every inch of his six-foot-four frame of sinew and honed muscle—leaning against the wall. The sides of his head were shaved, revealing a new tattoo on the left side of his skull—the Mac Tíre, our clan, was named for. He dipped his bearded chin in acknowledgment before his dark gaze skated back to the main stage.

I wound my way back to the bar and found Finnan waiting. Delux was hanging off him, her arms across his shoulders, while she pressed her tits up against his arm. Finnan's gaze locked on mine when he saw me, and he shrugged the girl off him. She stumbled back a step then stared—indignant—at Finnan.

"Don't," Mary warned from behind the bar. "Walk away, Delux. Now."

The woman blinked at the Pull, back to Finnan, then wandered off.

"Caolan told me about the missing delivery. Someone got to it before we could."

I nodded.

"This shite needs to be stopped, Grayson. We're looking

like a bunch of fucking children getting their toys taken off them. I didn't spend this long building the clan's reputation for it to be taken away by under-fucking-handed snitches stealing our shit."

"Understood."

He placed his glass of whisky down onto the bar with an audible *thunk*. "Do you? Because from where I'm fucking standing, you're doing shit. Get your fucking guys on it, and find out who the rat is!"

"I will," I swore.

He glared at me for a moment longer, then asked, "How's my fiancée?" The leer in his voice grated on my nerves. Like the fuck I could talk, though. I'd just let Rhapsody suck my cock while I thought of Sloane.

"The ketamine is almost completely out of her system. She seems fine."

"I'm looking forward to seeing her."

Something about the way he said that made me want to stake my claim on the girl, but I kept my trap shut. I had to remind myself—*again*—that she wasn't mine. "Where will you take her to dinner tomorrow?"

"The Alehouse. I want the rest of the clan to meet her." He eyed me. "I need her to be a fucking knock-out. Is she as pretty in real life as she is in photographs?"

A thousand times more. "Aye."

"Good. I don't need to be bedding a dog." Wrapping his fingers around the glass of whisky, he drained the liquid and stood, buttoning his jacket. "You sparring tomorrow?"

My free hand curled into a fist, and I wanted nothing more than to take a swing at Finnan. Sparring was the way to make that happen. "Aye," I rasped, my tone more severe than I wanted it to be.

He nodded. "Good. I need you to stay with Sloane. Continue guarding her with your life, Grayson."

I swallowed roughly. Going to the club tonight with Sloane was going to be difficult. "What about you?"

"I have Shay with me." He stepped around me, then said, "Don't let that girl out of your sight, Kent. I've given up too much to have her."

6

SLOANE

AS SOON AS GRAYSON HAD LEFT, I'D GIVEN IT a minute, then thrown my shoulders back and opened the apartment door. Two men with machine guns were standing guard. One of them turned and looked at me, flashing me a gold-toothed smile. He had tattoos all over his face and, from what I could see, most of his body. I retreated from the door, locked it, then studied my surroundings. The apartment was still as cold as a morgue and just as boring. Falling back onto the training dear-old-dad had given me, I searched the apartment, starting in the kitchen.

Pulling open the peninsular island's drawers, I was hoping to find a knife, but there were none—not even a butter knife. The cooktop was electric, so no naked flames. Moving into the living room, all the furniture was either too heavy for me to pick up and wield or bolted to the floor. The bathroom mirror—although glass—was safety glass that would only crumble when broken.

When I discovered that all the bedrooms had the same bolted-down furniture, I finally understood. They were keeping weapons away—not so I could use them against someone else, but to use them on me. There were no options here.

Resigned, I pulled open the closet door and found the racks and shelves filled with clothes. Clothes all in my size.

"What fresh hell is this?" I muttered to myself, pushing things aside to get a better look at the clothing. They were all the kinds of things I wore back at home. I let the clothing fall back together, wondering if I'd had someone watching and reporting back on me for a while now, but neither me nor my father and his men had noticed.

In a rush, I went to the white mirrored tallboy and yanked open the top drawer. It was filled with La Perla panties and bras, all with the price tags still on them. The next drawer down contained teddies and camisoles that I guessed were for sleeping.

The rest of the drawers contained folded t-shirts with designer labels and pairs of equally expensive jeans.

Glancing down at my filthy feet, I wondered whether footwear had been included in the wardrobe transplant. Back in the closet, I found six boxes of shoes—ranging from street shoes to Louboutins. I pulled out the pair of LBs. They were open-toe pumps with a heart-shaped heel detail and a sky-high hundred-millimeter heel. The inside of the footbed had cartoon-style pin-up girls in skimpy lingerie—all done on a red background the same color as the soles.

Fuck, these shoes had to be worth over a thousand dollars in the States. I placed them back into their box, then slid on the lid.

I stood there—stunned—for a moment before deciding that I had to do *something*. I was still a mess from the earlier vomiting incident, and if I was going out tonight, I needed to at least put in some effort.

I opened the door of the en suite bathroom, and I could only describe it in one word… luscious. The white marble was veined with gold like the builder or designer had wanted to inject some sort of color or personality into the space. The walk-in shower had dual rain shower heads, with a double vanity and built-in medicine cabinets. I checked behind one and found a toothbrush, toothpaste, dental floss, and mouth wash. Inside one of the drawers in the vanity was an array of different hair brushes, as well as a case of Mac cosmetics.

Shaking my head, I turned on the faucets in the shower and was stunned to feel that the temperature was almost perfect right away. Stepping away, I stripped out of the oversized t-shirt, then hooked my thumbs into the waistband of the panties. I shimmied out of them, leaving the scrap of fabric on top of the shirt.

I turned but paused when I caught my reflection in the mirror. I looked washed out, and with hair the color of mine, looking washed out meant my skin had a blueish tinge to it. Already pale skin mixed with nausea and vomiting equaled an ethereal specter.

Getting into the shower, I ducked my head under the spray and let the water wash away all the dirt and grime of the last however long. I had no idea how long it had been since I was taken, but it couldn't have been any longer than twenty-four hours—more than likely a lot less than that.

I brushed my teeth and flossed, all while the water beat down on me from above. The pressure was sublime, easing away aches in my shoulders and back that I hadn't realized I had. I could only blame it on being laid out unconscious for long periods of time.

Rinsing out my mouth, I tipped my head back and soaked through my hair once more. Wiping the water from my eyes, I scanned the in-built shelf in front of me and grabbed the bottle of shampoo. Squeezing a quarter-sized amount into my palm, I lathered up my hair and rinsed. After I put the conditioner in to sit, I washed and scrubbed until my skin was pink, then did the final rinse of my hair.

When I stepped from the shower, I wrapped myself in a towel, then grabbed another for my hair. A waft of sandalwood-scented steam filled the spacious bathroom, and I tried not to think about how Grayson smelled exactly the same.

After drying off, I padded back into the bedroom and opened the closet. I suspected it would be cold outside, so I selected a pair of dark-wash skinny jeans and a soft gray bralette top to wear under a chunky white sweater.

Pulling open the top drawer, I scanned the contents and decided on a lace triangle bra in pale violet and a matching set of sheer Brazilian panties. As I leaned forward to secure the bra, I wondered who had decided on the different sets. Had they sent another woman to do the shopping, or had a man selected everything. Judging by how transparent and skimpy they were, I was betting on a man.

My mind made the leap that maybe Grayson had been the one to purchase everything in my wardrobe, but I dismissed it immediately. He didn't seem like the kind of man who would do such a thing.

Once I had the bra and panties in place, I stepped into the jeans and secured the bralette top.

Unwinding the towel from my head, I ran my fingers through it before opening the bottom cupboards in the bathroom in search of a hair dryer.

I found one along with a hair straightener.

Both devices went onto the marble counter, and I began drying then straightening my hair. When I was finished, my platinum hair looked like a sheet of satin falling down my back. A lot of people thought I got the color of my hair from a bottle, but after seeing my mom, I knew I'd gotten it from her.

Switching off and unplugging the dryer and straightener, I pulled out the cosmetics and applied a light base, highlighted my sharp cheekbones, and applied a smoky eye to make the color of my eyes pop.

By the time I was done, I looked and felt more like myself again. Exiting the bathroom, I walked back down the hallway, drawing to an abrupt stop, when I saw Grayson leaning a hip against the kitchen counter with his arms folded and his blue eyes dark with lust.

7

GRAYSON

KEEP YOUR EYES OFF HER FUCKING LEGS, YOU *god-damn cocksucker!*

Even though I'd told myself this before, it was worth repeating. My gaze shifted to her face for a moment before going back to trace her body, starting at her bare feet and working their way up. She'd slipped into one of the pairs of jeans I'd picked out for her, along with an oversized cream sweater. The sheer bulk of the sweater made her already small frame look smaller, but I fucking liked that. I liked it when a woman was smaller than I was. It called to something primal within me—some urge to protect at all costs.

When I got to her chest, I wondered whether she had on one of the lingerie sets I'd bought. Yeah, I bet she fucking did.

As soon as that thought registered, though, I shoved

it away. I was not supposed to be mentally undressing my boss's future wife.

Her hair had been straightened, and as she moved, I caught the scent of the expensive shampoo that I'd left in the bathroom.

I must've been staring too long, though, because she folded her arms and glared at me.

"You got a problem with what I'm wearing?" she asked.

"No." I'd showered and changed too, and judging by the way her eyes had roved my body when she stepped into the room, she liked what she saw.

"Where are we going?"

"To a club."

Her eyes widened. "I can't get into a club. I'm only eighteen."

I suppressed a laugh. "Eighteen is the legal age in Ireland, lass. You can get into a club, go to a bar, buy alcohol. Whatever you want."

She gave me a slow-eyed blink like she couldn't believe what I'd just said was true. "Seriously?"

"Seriously. Are you ready?" I eyed her sweater. "You got anything under that?"

Her eyes narrowed on my face. "What?"

"We're going to a nightclub, lass," I repeated. "It's going to be hot, sweaty, and dark."

She raised her chin a little and said, "I'm going to get changed."

When she emerged twenty minutes later, I had to pick my jaw up off the floor. She was in the black, long-sleeved halter dress I'd bought on a fucking whim because I wanted to see her in it but never thought she'd wear it. I'd been watching Sloane for too fucking long. That was the reason Finnan had asked me to fill her wardrobe—because I'd been surveilling her in Detroit on and off for the past six months.

I knew she was a jeans and sneakers kind of woman, but also one who enjoyed getting dressed up for dinners and going to the theater.

The dress she was wearing was skin-tight through the hips, the fabric clinging to her slight curves. The top part of the dress was two panels that crossed over near the top of her throat, revealing a tantalizing keyhole of her breasts. Sheer black sleeves covered her arms, leaving her back exposed.

On her feet were the pair of black patent calfskin leather shoes with a fifteen-centimeter heel. The Louboutin's had cost more money than most people made in a week over here, but seeing them on her, was totally worth it. The red lining on the sole flashed with every step she took, and I knew that her calves would look amazing as she walked in front of me.

"Fuck me." This woman was getting to me.

She glanced down at herself. "Isn't this more fitting for a club?"

It was, but keeping other men away from her was going to be a fucking issue. I must've taken too long to answer because she turned and called over her shoulder, "Why are you stroking your gun?"

I glanced down to find that I was indeed stroking it. "Just thinking about all the men who'll be trying to get close to you."

She frowned like she couldn't quite understand what I'd said. "I'll get changed."

"No. Don't." *Fuck.* "You look…" *Amazing. Edible. Fuckable.* "Fine. You look fine."

One of her pale brows winged up. "Fine?"

"Yeah."

Her mouth compressed into a thin line. "Fine," she muttered. She threw her shoulders back and walked to the door. I let her go because I wanted to see if I was right about her calves.

And I fucking was.

She stepped out into the hallway, her head turning from one side of the door to the other as she saw the two men guarding her apartment. She gave each of them a slight, confident nod and walked toward the elevator bank. As I stepped from the apartment, both sentinels straightened their spines and rolled their shoulders back.

In Gaelic, I told them, "Don't leave her apartment unattended. We'll be back in a few hours."

When I turned back around, Sloane was staring at me. She opened her mouth as if she wanted to argue, then shut it. Keeping the smirk off my face, I reached around her and punched at the down button on the panel. She stiffened at my proximity, and this close, I could smell her natural vanilla scent underneath the scent of the shampoo she'd used.

Against all my better judgment, I lingered there for a moment longer before straightening and folding my hands in front of my body. Sloane turned her head slightly as if she wanted to keep me in her periphery while we waited.

The elevator car arrived, sending the doors open with a soft *whoosh*. Stepping inside, I scanned every corner—more out of habit rather than any real danger—motioning for Sloane to follow me. I pushed the button for the basement level, then rested against the metal wall.

Sloane heaved a sigh but didn't relax one bit. "Where are we going tonight?"

"A club called Foundry."

"Is it just you and me?"

"No. We're meeting my sister there."

She half turned toward me. "The woman you were on the phone to when we were in the car?"

I nodded. "Fallon."

Facing me fully, she asked, "Older or younger? Probably younger right since you offered to go out with her."

"Right."

"How old is she?"

"Twenty-one."

"Have you always looked after her?"

Her question made me blink. "What makes you ask that?"

Her slender shoulders moved in a shrug, drawing my attention back to the creamy slope of her neck, the keyhole peek of her high and tight breasts. "You're a classic sigma."

"Run that by me again, lass?"

Her lips quirked up a little in the corner. "A sigma. It's a personality type."

Folding my arms over my chest, I decided to goad her a little to see if she had any fire. "Did you read that in one of your female magazines?"

"Female magazines?"

"Yeah, like *Xposé. Image. Woman's Way.*"

She cocked her head to one side. "*Woman's Way?*"

"It's a fashion and beauty magazine."

She laughed at me then, the sound of it stoking the low-level simmer of my growing lust for her. "More like *Cosmopolitan*. But no. I took a college intro to psychology class my last semester of school."

I shifted my weight to cross one foot over the other. Fuck, I think I liked her even more for that. She was smart and not afraid to show it. "All right, so you learned it in a psych class. What is a sigma personality?"

"They're intimidating and self-assured, completed devoted and loyal to those they value, but are also utterly elusive."

"Sounds about right."

"They also have the ability to be vulnerable," she tacked on, staring at me.

I said nothing to that because the elevator cruised to a stop, and the doors opened. I glanced up from Sloane's face to look out at the half dozen men waiting for us. Beyond the mass of guns and muscle was the same black Range Rover as before. I stepped out. Torin was leaning against the front quarter panel, but as soon as he saw me, he straightened. I watched as his dark eyes went from me to Sloane, who had stepped up beside me.

Torin's jaw unhinged. He wasn't even trying to fucking hide that he was staring. Biting the inside of my cheek, I stepped in front of Sloane and broke his line of sight.

Torin's eyes went back to my face, and he had the grace to look like a kid who just got caught with his hand in the cookie jar.

He made a quick cutting motion with his hand, and I turned around to see the other men staring at Sloane's ass.

"She's your motherfucking boss's future wife," I growled, hustling Sloane toward the rear door.

Too bad I couldn't remember that fucking fact.

Torin got with the fucking program and hustled to get the door open in time for Sloane to slide across the seat. On purpose, I stood in front of the opening so none of the other men could see her accidentally flash her panties. When she was settled, I got in too, then slammed the door.

In the silence of the car, her vanilla scent overwhelmed me.

"You can let go of my hand now," she said softly.

I tore my gaze from the window. "What?"

She gestured to where her hand was on the seat between us, to where my fingers were threaded with hers. I jerked away, flexing my fingers.

"Sorry. I didn't…"

"Realize," she finished for me. "I know. You gripped my hand at the same time as you realized all the guards were staring."

Turning to face her fully, I asked, "You were aware."

"Of course I was. I've been stared at my whole life."

"Somehow, that thought doesn't make me feel any better," I grumbled.

"People have recognized who I was since before I was a pre-teen. People stare. I'm Aidan Kavanaugh's only daughter. I'm the mafia princess of Detroit."

"I don't think you need a prince to rescue you."

"I don't."

Torin had gotten into the driver's seat and started the engine. It went from a loud roar to a purring prowl as he accelerated out of the parking garage and into the rain-drenched streets of Galway. It was barely even eight o'clock in the evening—too early to be heading to a club—but I wanted to make sure Sloane ate a decent meal since Finnan had to cancel.

When we pulled up in front of a restaurant on Fairgreen Road, she turned to me and asked, "This is the nightclub?"

"No. This is a Michelin Star restaurant."

"You have a reservation?"

"No."

"Then how—"

"Sloane, your father was known by sight in Detroit, right?"

"Yes."

"Well, I'm known by sight here in Galway."

I thought she was going to start arguing with me, but she simply bit her lip and looked down. "I'm over-dressed."

"You're perfect."

Her head jerked up like it was on strings, and she stared at me. I stared right back, taking in every inch of her beauty. She'd gone heavier on her eye makeup, making her pale gray irises pop. Her lips were done in a nude color, her skin perfect and unblemished.

Sloane snapped out of the moment when Torin opened the door with an umbrella held over the opening and stepped to the side. He'd reached into his jacket to touch his Glock, ready to draw if someone so much as sneezed on her. I got out the other side, my gaze sweeping the street as I buttoned up my jacket and moved to the other side of the car. Torin was standing in front of Sloane now, his head moving as his eyes watched.

I reached for Sloane's hand, then hesitated. Touching her could become addictive. I could sense that, but I still wanted to feel her soft skin against my palm. In the end, I flexed my hand into a fist and opened the door of the restaurant, letting Torin lead her in.

"Be back here at nine-thirty," I told him in Gaelic, then turned my attention to the hostess station. A woman in her mid-thirties greeted us.

"Welcome, Mr. Kent. It's a pleasure to see you again. Your table is ready."

She led the way through the restaurant, which was decorated in natural timber with warm yellow lights overhead. Our table was secluded and quiet—far enough away from other diners, some of which had stared openly at the beautiful woman I was leading through the restaurant.

The thought that Finnan would soon see this reaction made me want to stab something.

I pulled out Sloane's chair for her, waiting until she was settled in before sliding it forward. She turned her head slightly, so her warm breath feathered across my hand as I held onto the chair back.

"Thank you."

"You're welcome, lass," I replied softly.

Stepping away from her, I rounded the table and sat

down. A waiter appeared a moment later, handing us the menus. "Welcome to—"

I stopped him. "The chef knows what to prepare for us," I told him.

"Of course, Mr. Kent." He nodded to me, then to Sloane, before disappearing.

Sloane's eyes were alight with humor. "And I thought my father was abrupt and arrogant."

"Arrogant? You think I'm arrogant?"

She gestured in the direction the waiter had gone. "You don't think talking to him like that, then dismissing him was rude?"

"No."

"You just expect people to do what you say."

"Aye."

Her platinum hair fell over her shoulder as she shook her head. "You're just like my father."

"If you think I'm arrogant, lass, wait until you meet Finnan."

She pursed her lips. "What does he look like?"

"Finnan?"

She nodded.

Sitting back in the chair, I stretched my legs out under the table and thought about how I would describe my boss. "He's got dark hair, a beard. He's a few inches shorter than me."

"Is he built like you?"

"No."

She wrapped her arms around herself. "How old is he? I don't want to be marrying a guy who's ancient. I don't want to have to open my legs for him."

"Twenty-nine."

Her eyes widened. "So young?"

"He came into power after his father was assassinated."

"How long ago was that?"

"Nine years."

"He was only twenty when he became head of the mafia?"

"Not the head of all the Irish mafia, lass. The Irish aren't organized like the Italians in the US. Or even the American-Irish. There are clans all over the country. Each of them runs independently."

"If that's true, how in the hell did I become part of a deal between Finnan and my father?"

"They had a private arrangement." The truth was, I had no idea how it had all come about.

Before she could ask any more questions, a waitress appeared with a bucket of champagne on ice, placing it next to the table. With a flourish, she set the champagne flutes onto the table in front of us and offered to pour.

Sloane watched the golden liquid flow into the glass, and I—in turn—watched her. She looked amazing in this light—a soft glow of yellow. Her cheekbones were sharp, her nose perfectly proportioned. Her eyes were expressive, and her lips were plump and perfect. For a moment, I wondered what they'd taste like.

The waitress finished pouring and left us alone.

I shook my head and gestured to the glass in front of Sloane. "Taste it."

With a shaking hand, she reached out, wrapping her long

fingers around it. Bringing the rim to her mouth, she took a sip, her eyes closing as she savored the flavor.

Fuck, that made my dick hard.

"What do you think?" My voice was nothing but a rasp.

Her lids fluttered open, and she blinked a couple of times. "It's amazing."

I nodded and picked up my own glass, taking a sip and never taking my eyes off her.

"How did you join the Mac Tíre clan?"

She'd even got the pronunciation right—*mok cheer-a.*

Setting the champagne back onto the table, I thought about how much I wanted to tell her. Self-preservation told me not to expose too much, no matter how badly I wanted to spill everything.

"I never finished school. My da died when I was fifteen, and my ma had died of cancer the year before. It was just me and Fallon. I didn't want her to drop out of school, so I started looking for work. When I was sixteen, I started running errands for Finnan's father, Kellen. He saw that I was tall and strong, street-savvy too, and he took me under his wing, taught me how the world worked when you were looking at it through mob glasses."

"I'm sorry about your parents," Sloane whispered.

I jerked my head up to look at her, not realizing I'd been staring at the empty table in front of me to start with. "It was a long time ago, lass. Nothing to be sorry about."

"Still, I'm sorry. I know what it's like to lose a parent."

I asked a question I shouldn't have asked, "Your ma?"

She nodded once. "At least I thought she was dead. For the last eighteen years, I'd been told she was. Until..." She frowned as she thought. "How long has it been since I was abducted?"

My shoulders tensed. "Almost twenty-four hours."

Shaking her head, she continued, "Until about twenty-six hours ago when she showed up in my life, very much alive."

I thought back to the auction. To the woman who had the same platinum blonde hair and gray eyes. I'd thought she looked familiar at the time, but now that Sloane was talking about it, I realized *why* she looked so familiar.

"The woman who was with the man who bought you at the auction, she's your ma?"

Sloane lifted her chin by way of answering. "She'd come to rescue me from my father's evil plan to sell me in a flesh auction. She and Dagger had saved me, but then *you* showed up."

The waiter reappeared with four plates balanced on his hands and forearms. While he was placing them down on the center of the table, another waiter set some empty plates in front of us.

When everything had been unloaded, the waiter stood up straight and announced, "Tonight, the chef has prepared for you two different tasting plates. One is what's available now, and the other is a new menu that has yet to be rolled out to diners."

I watched Sloane's face as he rattled off the contents of each plate, enjoying the way her eyes widened with each course. By the time the waiter walked away, she glanced over at me and smiled.

"You enjoy dining out," I told her.

"I do." Her gaze traveled over the four plates between us. She picked up the squid while I tried a beef dish.

As we ate, I carefully cataloged each of her expressions, quickly learning that when she enjoyed something, her eyes fluttered shut. When something was sour, she wrinkled her nose. When she didn't like something at all, her mouth flexed into a grimace—but only for a second—before she smoothed her expression out into a pleasant sort of passivity.

After the plates were empty and cleared away, I ordered a selection of desserts we could share.

She picked up her champagne flute and finished what was left in her glass. "That was delicious."

"Wait until you try their tiramisu. It's better than what you can find in Italy."

Setting down her glass, she glanced around the restaurant. It was quieter than when we walked in, people finishing their meals and leaving to either see a play, go to a club or simply return home.

"Where's the restroom?"

I jerked my chin to the other side of the room.

She rose from her seat, folding her napkin and leaving it beside her plate. As soon as she was gone from the table, one of the sentinels who had come in after us rose from his seat and followed her. He nodded at me as he passed.

Five minutes later, she was back, and she did not look happy.

"A guard? Really?"

"You noticed him then?"

"Of course, I did. He might as well have a huge sign over

his head that says he's one of your men."

"Rafferty isn't known for his conspicuousness."

"Well, *Rafferty*, scared the pants off a woman who walked into the bathroom right after me. Made her wait until I was finished before letting her in."

"Standard operating procedure. He had to make sure nobody had access to you." I eyed her. "And to make sure you didn't escape."

"Someone else could've already been in there," she replied, balling her hands into fists.

I liked the way her cheeks pinked up when she was angry. The minute I thought it was the minute I forced it from my head. "I have another one of my men sweeping the bathroom every ten minutes. It was empty."

Her pale brows rose. "How do you even know that?"

Shrugging, I said, "Because that's their job."

"Do you really think someone would try to harm me in the bathroom?"

"It's a possibility. Look… Finnan said to keep you safe. This is me keeping you safe. You don't like it? Take it up with him."

"Oh, I will," she seethed, folding her arms across her chest.

I smiled at her, enjoying the way she looked so damn fuckable when she was mad.

Our desserts came, but we ate them in silence. Just like before in the car, she was using the silent treatment on me. Fine by me. I always preferred actions over words, and she was showing me plenty of action by the way she glared at me, the tightness in her jaw, the set of her shoulders.

When it was clear she wasn't going to let it go, I rose from the table and offered her my hand. Ignoring the gesture, she stood and placed her napkin down beside her mostly empty plate.

She stepped clear of the table and walked toward the door. As we left the restaurant, she asked, "You're so arrogant you aren't even going to pay?"

"They have my card on record. They'll take care of it."

She blinked at me like she wasn't sure she'd heard me, then shook her head. "Where to now, then?"

"The club. My sister is waiting for us."

Right on cue, Torin pulled up in the Rover, and I opened the back door for Sloane. As she slid in, the hem of her dress rode up a little, flashing the top of her thigh nearly up to her hip bone.

Lord, help me.

I bit back the groan and slid in beside her.

8

SLOANE

WHEN THE DOOR SLAMMED SHUT, THE SMELL OF sandalwood and leather filled my nose. I had been able to smell it all through dinner, too, but now in this confined space, it was taking over my senses completely. I'd had a brief reprieve when I'd excused myself to go to the restroom, but any thoughts of escaping had been dashed when a man stepped from the end of the hallway, blocking the way.

We'd entered a sort of staring game, but I broke first when the other one of Grayson's men halted a fellow diner in her tracks, preventing her from using the restroom like a civilized human being.

"How far away is the club?" I asked.

"Not far," Grayson replied.

He was right. Only one block down, and we were there.

I turned to him. "Why in the hell didn't we just walk here?"

"This car is bulletproof," he pointed out. "You're not."

He stepped from the car while Torin ran around the hood to open my door. When he was in position, he opened it for me, and I stepped out into the road. Cars were creeping past to get by, and I had a feeling it was because Torin was flashing a firearm at them. He walked me around to Grayson, whose blue eyes were scanning the street. Without looking at me, he held out his arm, and I took it because that's what I was taught to do.

The fact that I hadn't accepted his hand in the restaurant was a testament to how pissed off I was with him.

Grayson gave Torin an order in Gaelic, then strode toward a building with a sign hanging above the door that said *Foundry*. There was a line of people that snaked around the front of the building then disappeared around the corner—all of them waiting to get in. Grayson, being Grayson, simply walked up to the bouncer and was let in.

I turned to glance at the people waiting. None of them looked pissed off that he'd cut. I guessed they'd take whatever shit he dished out because it was better than a fucking bullet in the head.

As we walked into the club, I had to let my eyes adjust to the dimness. I could feel the change in temperature instantly—the heat of sweaty bodies pressing against my skin. The air was stuffy and held the scents of too many different perfumes, colognes, and fresh sweat. There was a DJ at one end of the dancefloor bobbing his head to the music while strobe lighting and multicolored lasers pierced the darkness every now and again.

Grayson led us upstairs and to a part of the club that

was reserved for VIPs. He settled us into a deep eggplant-colored velvet booth that overlooked the dancefloor from a balcony, then hit a button in the middle of the table. A moment later, a server appeared with a bottle of champagne on ice. As she leaned down to place everything on the table, her black scoop-neck t-shirt gaped, flashing the tops of her breasts. I glanced at Grayson to see whether he would look, but his intense eyes were firmly on me.

Startled, I turned away. I'd noticed that he stared at me a lot. At the restaurant, while I was eating. Any time he thought I wasn't looking, he would stare. Instead of feeling creeped out by that, I found myself enjoying his attention, which was just another reason to think I was suffering from Stockholm Syndrome. One shouldn't find their captor handsome and mysterious.

And bangable.

So.

Fucking.

Bangable.

The server asked something, but I couldn't hear her over the music even though it was quieter up here.

Grayson said, "A dozen bottles of water."

The woman nodded and disappeared as quickly as she'd arrived.

He leaned forward and poured me a glass of champagne, but not one for himself. After he handed me the flute, I took a sip, needing something cool. The heat downstairs had been unbearable, but up here, we were close to a vent blowing cold air.

The champagne was the same as what we'd had in the

restaurant, and even though it was legal to drink here in Ireland, I still felt like I was breaking the law. While I sipped my drink, I stared out at the sea of people on the dance floor. The music playing now was fast and frenetic and not to my taste at all.

He tapped me on the shoulder, and I turned to find his face close to mine. I jerked back, but he pulled me close once more and said into my ear, "My sister just arrived with her friends. They're coming up here now."

"Okay." I sat back, taking another sip of my drink.

I noticed he wasn't drinking.

"Are you not having any champagne?"

He gave me serious eyes. "No. Not here."

I wanted to ask him why when a beautiful young woman with hair slightly lighter in color to Grayson's stepped past the velvet rope. In a navy-blue bodycon dress that hugged and clung to her every curve, I was slightly jealous of her. And when she threw her arms around Grayson's neck to hug him, that jealously flared more brightly.

Glancing away, I focused on the fact he was my kidnapper, and that helped to clear my thoughts.

"Sloane, this is my sister, Fallon," Grayson said.

Blinking from my thoughts, I remembered to smile at the other woman and offered her my hand. Instead of taking it, she drew me into a brief, friendly hug.

"It's so nice to meet you. Grayson's never introduced me to any of his girlfriends before."

"She's not my girlfriend," he said at the same time I replied, "I'm his captive."

"Oh." Eyes the same color as her brother's darted between

us. "It sounds like there's a lot to unpack there..."

Fallon barely batted an eyelash at my comment, which led me to think that she was well aware of who her brother worked for and what kinds of things they did.

"She's Finnan's fiancé," Grayson said. "I have to watch her."

"He has to make sure I don't escape," I added.

"Oh," Fallon repeated, then flashed me a brilliant smile before saying to Grayson, "Well, I'm just glad you could come out tonight, brother mine."

"It's been a while," Grayson agreed.

She turned and motioned two other women forward. "These are my friends, Molly and Sadie. Girls, this is my brother, Grayson, and Sloane."

Grayson said a gruff hello to the two other women who were staring at him like they'd just won the lottery. I peered up at the man and saw what they saw. Grayson was tall, built, and fucking gorgeous. The way he reacted to them was interesting though. Instead of lapping up the attention, he'd done exactly what a sigma personality would do. He withdrew and slid into that elusive mode they were well-known for. I wonder if he knew that his actions would only make the girls work harder for his attention.

"Where's Alana?" he asked his sister.

"She wasn't feeling well and bailed."

Grayson grunted and took a seat. Fallon took the spot next to me. Grayson was next to her until Molly squeezed in beside him and Fallon, while Sadie took the other side. With a smirk, I glanced over the top of Fallon's head to see Grayson staring down at the other two women with a look of thinly-disguised disdain on his face.

Turning my attention back to Fallon, I thought I'd get to know a little bit more about her, and by extension, Grayson.

"Can I get you a drink, Fallon?" I offered, leaning forward and grabbing the empty champagne flute.

She held up her hand like she was fending someone off. "Thank you, but no," she replied.

The waitress appeared with twelve bottles of water and placed them on the table. Grayson reached into his pocket and pulled out some cash and gave it to her. With a bob of her head, she left us to it.

Fallon leaned forward and took a bottle, and cracked the lid. Swallowing back half of the contents, she screwed the lid back on and looked around.

"Do you like to dance, Sloane?"

I did like to dance, but the words Grayson had said to me before rang in my head. He was probably right—men would be all over me if I went down there. Even as we'd walked through the main part of the club, there had been more than one roving hand. But this was too good of an escape opportunity to miss. With the crowds and the dim lighting, I would be able to slip away unnoticed, then get to a phone to call... not my father, but maybe I could reach my mother somehow.

Either way, I had to try.

"I probably shouldn't," I replied, gesturing to Grayson with my chin.

Fallon looked over at her brother. When she faced me again, she was grinning. "Gray is too distracted by my friends right now."

I peered over her shoulder to see him speaking to one of the women, his mouth close to her ear. Jealousy flared, stabbing me like a red-hot poker in the gut. *Why in the hell was I getting upset about this?*

"Come on." Fallon stood and held out her hand to me.

Another glance over at Grayson, and I saw my opportunity. Molly was all over him, practically climbing into his lap and trying to kiss him. I followed Fallon down to the dancefloor, checking out the possible escape routes on the way. There was a long hall with restrooms on the opposite side of the club. On the other side, behind the DJ, was a fire escape. The only other accessible way in and out was the front entrance.

I simply had to bide my time, despite the fleeting thought that Grayson would probably have stationed men all over this club keeping an eye on me. I wouldn't be able to get two feet before I was dragged back, but I had to try.

Before Fallon could step onto the dancefloor, I tugged on her hand and pointed to the restroom. She gave me a thumbs up, and I turned, intent on detouring right out the front door, but stopped when Fallon caught up with me.

"I thought you had to go to the loo," she yelled into my ear.

Fuck. "I do."

"I need to go, too. They're over here." She tugged me forward until we hit the hallway, where another five women were already waiting to relieve themselves.

We waited in silence for a few moments before I asked, "What do you do for work, Fallon?"

"I'm at nursing school," she replied. "First year of study."

"That's great. How's it going?"

"So far? Good. I'm sure things will get more difficult as the course goes on."

I nodded and shuffled up in the line.

"And what about you? You're Finnan's fiancé? How did you all meet?"

"We didn't," I replied. "I was sold to him."

Fallon pursed her lips. "I know what my brother does to make money. For a long time, I wasn't okay with it, but I realized that everything he does, he does it for the clan... and for me. To some of the men in this town, the clan is the only family they have. I mean, it's mine and Grayson's only family, so although I don't agree with the things they do, I know it's for the benefit of the clan and everyone in it."

What she was saying wasn't a foreign concept to me. My father had been the same way for a while. The members of the mafia were family.

"Finnan is a hard man, but he's also fair. He'd never mistreat you, but his patience isn't unending. If you push him too far, he will push back eventually."

The line moved up again. "He's like a lot of the men back home then. They have an antiquated way of looking at women. Their role is to have babies and look after the family."

"And the man's is to provide. It's the same here," Fallon said. "All I'm saying is that it could be worse."

Another half step along the wall and I was next. I peered up the hallway to see that there was a men's restroom a couple of feet away, then what appeared to be a janitor's closet. This was a dead end.

The restroom door opened, and I slipped inside the single cubicle, locking it behind me. There wasn't a window in there—nowhere for me to go. I didn't need to use the restroom, so I flushed after an appropriate amount of time, washed my hands, and stepped outside. Fallon smiled at me and stepped in, leaving me alone.

Now was my chance.

Bodies pressed against me as I pushed through, making a path to the door. Freedom was so close that I could smell the fresh air. Before I left, I risked one more glance over my shoulder. Nobody was there. I'd done it.

I stepped out...

... and ran straight into a firm body.

The scent of sandalwood and leather hit my nose, and I knew exactly who it was.

"Going somewhere, lass?" he asked in an amused drawl.

I stepped back, cupping my elbows in a vain attempt to keep warm. The wind was frigid here in Ireland. His icy eyes dropped to where I was hugging myself and his jaw flexed. "You should go back inside. It's cold."

"I'm fine," I replied, teeth beginning to chatter.

"You're not. Go inside now, or I'll take you in there myself."

I arched a brow. "You wouldn't dare."

He threw me over his shoulder without preamble, showing me how easy it was to manhandle me.

"Put me the fuck down!" I screamed, drawing the attention of some curious onlookers.

"No." Grayson's firm hand landed on my ass, slapping me into silence. My skin had warmed from his touch, and it had nothing to do with pain but fucking lust. I knew I was attracted to this man—my captor—but to be turned on with a single spank on the ass? Jesus, I was in more trouble than I thought.

I told him, "My ass is flashing to every man in here."

I felt more than heard his growl of disapproval. His warm palm came to cover my rear as he took me back upstairs, where we were alone. Lowering me onto the velvet cushion, he stared at me from only a few inches away.

"You're a fucking Neanderthal," I hissed.

He only stared at me as he took a seat opposite, crossing his leg at the ankle.

Exhaling loudly, I folded my arms under my breasts, making his eyes dart down. His mouth tightened. "That was the wrong thing to do, lass."

His voice was so deliciously dark.

"It was the right thing for me."

He sat forward, resting his elbows on his knees. "And what were you going to do, huh? Run for help? We *own* this city. Nobody would've helped you, or if they did, they would've returned you to Finnan."

Not letting him see my frustration, I said, "I would've called my mom."

"You have her number, do you?"

Fuck. "No, but there are other ways to get information."

He shook his head. "You don't get it, do you? You belong to the Mac Tíre clan now. Your life is not your own. It's Finnan's, and everything you do, every action you take, reflects on him." He crooked his finger at me, urging me closer.

Licking my lips, I did. God, help me, I did.

"The next time you run? I will personally punish you for the infraction."

9

GRAYSON

I DIDN'T KNOW WHY I'D THREATENED HER WITH punishment.

But as the words sat heavily between us, I could tell she was turned on by the idea. Maybe it was the firm slap I'd given her perfect ass. Was it still burning her skin? Still pebbling her nipples—hard and inviting—against the panel of her dress?

Fuck, that dress. Just as I'd assumed, men's tongues had rolled out of their mouths when she'd strolled into the club. She had no idea how close I was to pulling out my Glock and sharing around the bullets.

I was wound so tight, I was likely to fuck up the next man who even had a stray thought about her. My dick was as hard as a railway spike in my slacks. Did she know that I'd been hiding my hard-as-fuck erection from her all night?

I had to get a fucking grip. I'd become obsessed with her, and that obsession was starting to peek through.

"I need to go to the restroom," she announced, standing quickly.

Like hell I was going to let her attempt another escape. I grabbed her wrist before she could take more than two steps.

Her gaze swung back to me, her cheeks high with color. "You can't stop me from using the restroom."

"No, I can't, but given your proclivity to Shawshank it, I'm coming with you this time."

"You mean you don't have any of your men around here watching things like you did in the restaurant?"

I shook my head. Keeping tabs on her in a place like this was nearly impossible. I'd known that before deciding to bring her. "There's a ladies' room on this level," I told her, stepping clear of the table. "I'll show you."

With my hand cupping her elbow, I directed her down a short hallway that had been hidden by dark drapes. The lights were low in the confined space, barely illuminating the two doors near the end. Directing her into the first, I pushed open the door and followed her in.

Realizing what was happening, she spun around to face me. "What the hell?"

"I have to have eyes on you twenty-four-seven, lass." I let myself stare at her—uninhibited and unafraid of being caught. I let her see how much I wanted to touch her. "You've proven yourself untrustworthy."

"Fuck you."

I locked the door then smiled, but there was nothing

happy about it. It was predatory—I knew that—but I wanted her to see the beast she had brought to life. I darted my eyes to the cubicle behind her. "You said you needed the bathroom. I suggest you go while you have the chance."

For the first time, she looked unsure of herself before she lifted her chin—defiant. "Wait outside."

"No."

"I'm not using the restroom while you're standing here."

I folded my arms across my chest and leaned casually against the wall, even if my blood was humming with lust. "Well, I'm not leaving, lass, so I'd say we're at an impasse."

Throwing me a glare, she stomped inside the cubicle and shut the door. "Block your ears," she commanded.

"What?"

"Cover your ears," she hissed. "I don't need you to hear me pee."

Humoring her, I said after a moment, "Okay. Covered."

There was a long pause, then the sound of her relieving herself. After she flushed and the door unlocked, I pretended to lower my hands when she appeared. She sashayed to the sink on the opposite wall and washed her hands, carefully drying them afterward.

"Why are you looking at me like that?" she asked, glaring at me from the corner of her eye.

"Like what?"

"Like I *amuse* you or something."

"Maybe you do."

At this statement, she rolled her eyes, pitching the damp paper towel into the trashcan. I stalked closer, and her nostrils flared.

Her gaze dropped to my mouth briefly. "What are you doing?" Her indignation would've had stronger legs to stand on if she hadn't just stared at my mouth like a starving woman.

"Testing a theory."

She retreated a step. "What theory?"

"The theory that you enjoyed that spank I gave your arse before."

She barked a laugh, but the heat currently flushing the side of her neck told me that her amusement was the result of being turned on. Her nipples beaded to sharp points once more, and my mouth began to water. I wanted to have my mouth over them so badly. To tongue them. To make her squirm.

I crowded her against the marble counter, planting my hands on either side to hold her captive against my hard body. A shuddered breath escaped her, whispering across the skin of my neck. "You're trying to tell me you didn't enjoy it?"

She swallowed and looked away, only meeting my eyes once more when I tucked two fingers beneath her chin and tilted her face up to meet mine.

"You want to feel my warm hand against your fucking perfect arse again, don't you? You want that sting. That delicious erotic heat." I inched forward, my mouth hovering over hers. She licked her lips in anticipation. "All you have to do is say the word, Sloane, and I will happily spank you until your panties are soaked, and you're begging for my cock to be buried deep inside you."

I ran the tip of my finger over the elegant swoop of

her collarbones, down between her breasts, then flattened my hand over her chest, right where her heart thumped restlessly against my palm. "Is that the kind of punishment you'd like to receive?" My voice was low. Graveled. I was so turned on my dick pressed against the zipper of my slacks with increasing pressure. I knew I would never get inside this woman. Hell, I shouldn't even be enclosed in a private space with her, but with her looking at me like she was, I didn't give a fuck that she was Finnan's future wife.

I trailed my eyes down her body then met her gaze once more. "Tell me you want that, Sloane."

She squirmed but said nothing.

My hand flexed where it rested. Just a little more to the right, and I could have my hands over her perfect breast, abrading her taut nipple. I was standing on the edge of an incredibly dangerous cliff. One more touch and I would be crossing the line—touching what wasn't mine. Would Sloane keep our secret, or would she broadcast it to the world like she seemed to have no problem doing earlier with Fallon?

Her breathing was erratic, her chest heaving under my touch. Somehow, I found the strength to break the connection and stepped back. She stared at me with heavy-lidded eyes and a slack mouth.

It was time for me to get her the fuck home and away from me.

"I'm going to tell Fallon we're leaving," I said, taking another step back and breaking the spell even more.

"We're leaving?"

I nodded. "Yeah." I rubbed my mouth with the hand that

still lingered with the heat of her arousal. "I can't trust myself alone with you. Come on."

After she had grabbed her purse, I took her by the arm and led her to the dancefloor. I found Fallon dancing with Molly and Sadie. I'd had my doubts about my sister's recovery and whether coming out to a club was a good idea in the first place. But seeing her here tonight reminded me of a time before her addiction when she could have good, clean fun.

I pulled my sister to the side. "I have to take Sloane home," I told her. "Are you coming?"

She asked the girls what they wanted to do, and the answer was to stay a little longer.

"I don't want you leaving here alone, Fallon. After I take Sloane back, I'll come and get you. I'll be an hour."

She wrapped her arms around my body and hugged me. "Thanks for trusting me, Gray."

I dropped a kiss on her forehead. "I'll see you soon."

Tugging Sloane out the door, we stepped free of the sound and heat, and the Galway air felt almost electric against my face. Sloane inhaled deeply and let it out as the Rover pulled up to the curb.

Opening the rear door, I waved Sloane in, then climbed in after her.

"Why does she look like she's thinking of cutting off your balls and cramming them down your throat?" Torin asked me in Gaelic through the rearview mirror.

I glanced at the woman in question. That description matched well to the expression on her face. "Because I suspect she does," I replied back in Gaelic.

Sloane made a derisive sound down low in her throat, leaned forward and slid off her shoes. I spent way too long studying her athletic calves. *Fuck, she was too much of a distraction.*

In Gaelic, I barked at Torin, "Drive."

Torin drove through Galway like we were being chased, which was par for the course with him. When we finally turned into the parking garage for Sloane's apartment, he eased off the accelerator, letting the car coast down to the security gate. Once we were through, the half a dozen guards at the bottom of the elevator straightened. The Rover came to a smooth stop, and I got out. Torin did the same, standing in front of Sloane's door and waiting for my signal.

At my nod, he opened her door and kept her body covered with his as we walked to the elevator. I pressed the call button, and the doors slid open smoothly. Sloane stepped inside and I followed.

Before the doors could slide shut, I said, "We're going back to the club to get my sister. Standby."

He nodded, then turned his back as the doors slid shut.

Reaching across Sloane, I pushed the button for her floor, awareness sparking through my body with the proximity. She sucked in a sharp breath, but that was the only indication she'd felt anything. Tension filled the elevator car, the sexual energy swirling until it reached a fever pitch.

The elevator doors sprang open. Half a dozen guards lowered their weapons from where they were aimed at our chests and returned to their positions against the wall. Sloane walked out of the elevator car ahead of me, opening her apartment door and then attempting to slam it shut behind her. With a growl, I pushed inside and followed her into the living room.

Her gray eyes were bright with anger as she spun to face me. She was a furious tempest, a storm of emotions. So fucking beautiful that it hurt to breathe. My pulse was jackhammering in my throat—I wanted her. I wanted it so badly that my chest ached.

But she was Finnan's.

And I couldn't touch her.

"Stay here and stop being a pain in my arse," I barked.

Turning, I left the apartment, slamming the door shut behind me.

"Nobody in or out," I told the guards, my anger curling out with my words. I was looking for a release for all this energy I had in me. The ride back down to the garage was stifled, and when I stepped out, all my men took one look at my face and got busy glancing around at anything else.

It was only Torin who was brave enough to ask, "Ready to go?"

For just a moment, I considered getting back into the elevator and going back up to Sloane's apartment, but she was as off-limits as anyone could get. If Finnan knew what was going through my head about this bride-to-be—if he knew how perverted my thoughts were—he would put me down.

Permanently.

So, instead of following through with what I *wanted* to do, I forced my feet into motion and walked the few feet to the car. Torin shut the door behind me, and I exhaled.

I'd done it. I'd walked away. But…

I inhaled and smelled her—her scent lingering in the interior.

"Jesus *fuck*," I grumbled, holding my head in my hands and shutting my eyes. I took in one more breath, then opened my eyes to find myself staring at the Louboutins she'd slipped off her feet. Reaching down, I picked up one shoe and studied it.

She'd probably want them returned.

I should take them back to her.

"I need a minute," I said to Torin.

Scooping up the other black stiletto, I opened the rear door and stepped from the car. The elevator doors were still open, so I rushed inside and pushed the button for Sloane's floor. I'd just leave them inside the door. At least, that's what I told myself I'd do until I actually reached her apartment. Then all I wanted to do was open it and see her one last time.

I tried the handle and found the door unlocked. My blood pressure went through the roof, my anger finally having somewhere to go. Yanking open the door, I stepped into the apartment and startled Sloane, who was standing in the kitchen with a tub of ice cream in one hand and a spoon in the other.

Her anger made her eyes darken. Jamming the spoon inside the carton, then slamming it onto the counter, she demanded, "What the hell do you think you're doing barging in here without knocking?"

I stepped toward her. "What the hell do you think you're doing *not* locking your apartment door behind me?"

She gave me an exasperated look, rolling her eyes. Gesturing to the door, she said, "If you haven't noticed, I've got my own battalion out there guarding this place. If anyone got through all those thugs, then a locked door would hardly stop them. And why are you here? I thought we were done."

"We're far from done, lass."

Dropping the shoes, I took her by the wrist and pulled her into the line of my body. My primed, fucking-rock-hard body. Her mouth parted. Heat simmered in her gaze, and like a fucking moth to the flame, I wanted her more.

"You're playing a dangerous game, lass." The urge to mark her seemed to claw at my back, overtaking my common sense. My gaze tracked down her body. The dress—her fucking dress—taunted me. Spinning her around, I pressed her against the counter.

"Your fucking mouth always gets you into trouble. Hands down," I growled into her ear.

"No."

Twining her hair around my fist, I bit out, "Hands. Down. Now."

"Why?"

"Because even though I can't take you rough like I want to, I can do other things."

"L-l-like what?" she whimpered.

"I'm going to jerk off onto your beautiful arse. Cover it in my cum. Mark my fucking territory." I tightened my grip. "Hands down, Sloane."

I braced for the reminder that she was Finnan's fiancé, braced for the threat that she'd tell him, so when her delicate pink tongue darted out to moisten her lips and she placed her palms down onto the cool, white marble, I breathed out a sigh of relief. Triumphant, my dick twitched behind the zipper of my slacks, and anticipation coursed through me. With a hand between her shoulder blades, I pressed her forward so her back was straight, and her ass was raised. She laid with her cheek pressed to the cold stone, her gray eyes on me.

"Stay there."

I lifted the hem of her dress, sliding the clinging material up over her ass and settling it above her hips. Her violet panties were sheer. Lace. Half covering her glorious ass. I slapped one cheek, then the other, noticing how she shifted her weight, squeezing her thighs together.

"You like that, baby? I knew you enjoyed me turning your arse pink."

"I hate you." The words would've had more power if she hadn't mewled them while trying to find relief from the friction.

"Yeah, I bet you do." Unzipping my slacks, my cock sprang free of the confines. Gripping it at the base, I slid my hand up the hard length, unable to stop the groan that bubbled up from my throat. Sloane shifted restlessly on the spot. Her pussy was still hidden behind the lace of her panties, but I could see she was already wet.

"Is that cunt soaked?" I asked, releasing the tension on her hair.

Her eyes fluttered shut with the rush of endorphins. "Yes."

With a growl, I tore the panties from her waist, exposing

her fully to my view. The patches of skin on her ass—warm and pink—made me bite the inside of my cheek in anticipation.

"Let me feel how wet I've made you."

She widened her stance, making room for my hand to slide through her folds. I collected as much of her arousal as I could before bringing it to my cock and gliding her juices up and down. Lubricated by her desire, I increased my pace, twisting my wrist at the end and sending sparks of lust through me.

Sloane shifted uneasily, her breath puffing out of her and misting onto the marble beneath her cheek. Her arm shifted, and I caught movement between her legs. She was rubbing her clit, getting herself off to *me* getting off on her ass. A groan broke free from my throat when her fingers increased their pace.

My balls tightened as I felt my release coming. Knowing I was going to be unloading on all that soft skin shoved me over the edge. Stepping closer, I grabbed hold of her hip, keeping her in place as I came. The first drop of liquid landed on the crease of her ass and slid down into the valley between her cheeks.

Sloane moaned, then jerked forward as she came on her fingers. A loud moan punctuated the space between us, and I shoved my hand over her mouth to stop the noise from carrying. Knowing I was physically stopping the sound of her pleasure made me see stars as I shuddered through my own release until finally looking up.

Sloane's ass and lower back were painted in opaque puddles, many of which had begun to drip down her backside. Standing slowly, I snapped the dishtowel from the handle of the oven and began cleaning her up.

While she was still bent over, I rasped into her ear, "I'm going to taste that cunt of yours next time. I need to have all that honey dripping down my throat as I tongue-fuck your pussy."

10

SLOANE

I'M GOING TO TASTE THAT CUNT OF YOURS NEXT time. *I need to have all that honey dripping down my throat as I tongue-fuck your pussy.*

I bit my lip to stop the moan, but the erotic picture was too much. My body hadn't yet cooled from the rush of heat that had shot through me when Grayson had told me—in no uncertain terms—what he wanted to do to me.

Even now—hours later—I could feel his cum searing the skin on my ass, the pulsing of my inner walls as I came so hard in the knowledge that he couldn't help himself.

The man who thought he had complete control had bent. *To me.*

Squeezing my legs together, I shoved the quilt from my too-hot body, letting the cold morning air kiss all that flushed skin. After that declaration, he'd left the apartment, promising he'd be back this morning with Finnan. I had no idea what time that would be, but it would be soon.

Without warning, the bedroom door opened, and a man dressed in a two-piece suit filled the jambs.

I could only assume this was my husband-to-be.

Finnan Quinn was tall—almost six-feet—only slightly shorter than Grayson. His hair was dark, except for one streak of white running through it. His scruffy beard was the same dark color as his hair.

Green eyes swept down my body, causing me to tug the blankets back into place. When his gaze returned to my face, his top lip curled into a smile. "Drop the blanket, lass." He approached the bed. "I want to see what I got from my end of the deal."

I tensed. "Deal?"

"Aye. With your father." He studied my face impassively. "Drop the blankets."

"No."

His dark brows rose, and when he next spoke, his voice was terrifyingly sharp and threatening. "No?"

I swallowed roughly. "That's right. No."

Finnan shook his head, an unpleasant smile on his face that chilled me down to my bones. "I gave up another deal to have you. Get out of that fucking bed and undress. I want to know that it was worth my while."

Clutching the quilt more closely to my chest, I asked, "What deal?"

Irritation flared in his green eyes. Then, with a low snarl, he stepped forward and yanked the quilt from the bed—from my body—exposing the navy-blue silk camisole and matching shorts to his eyes. His gaze darkened as he stared at my near-nakedness, traveling over the long length of my legs, my hips before lingering on my chest. The cold air had made my nipples pucker, so I folded my arms across them, hiding them from view.

"I expect obedience from my wife. Loyalty." His hungry gaze tracked down to between my legs. "The sooner you accept that, the better it'll be for you."

Through gritted teeth, I said, "I assume I can expect the same from you?" When he cocked his head to the side as if listening, I continued, "If I become your wife, I'll expect your loyalty too. I damn well will *not* share my husband with another woman."

Finnan's shoulders stiffened. It probably didn't happen too often that a woman—or anyone—answered back. When he finally spoke, it was low and menacing. "You don't know how things work here, lass, so I'll give you a pass this one time." He turned and looked at me, his green eyes going cold. "But if you ever presume to tell me what to do again, if you talk back to me, I'll find another use for you… one where you won't get a say in who sticks his dick in you."

He left the room, leaving the bedroom door ajar. Outside, there was an angry exchange in Gaelic, then the apartment door slammed shut.

I glared at the floor—my breathing erratic and heavy—as anger churned through me. With my hands curling into fists, I counted to ten, each exhalation marking the next ascending number.

From the doorway, there was a bass growl. My eyes flew open, and I found Grayson standing there. His words from the night before whispered seductively through my mind. He stared at me, his irises being completely swallowed by his pupils. He was dressed in a pair of jeans so faded they were almost white and a black t-shirt that strained across his biceps and torso. I let my gaze skim down his body until I saw the huge bulge behind his zipper.

I could've yanked the quilt back up—that was my first instinct—but I didn't want to. My nipples hardened at the memory of Grayson pulling my hair, dominating me, and coming all over my ass. And when his ravenous gaze darted to my chest, my lips parted on a gasp. A thrill of lust licked through my blood at the heavy look in his eyes.

He took a step closer, kicking the door shut behind him. For the longest time, he remained there, breathing heavily, his hands bunching into fists every few seconds. We were frozen in that tableau until he crooked his finger at me.

As if I was a puppet on invisible strings, I got off the bed and went to him. Wrapping his hand around the back of my neck, his strong fingers pressed against my skull, making me feel suddenly boneless. His other hand skimmed along the front of my neck, cupping my jaw gently. I was held immobile in his large grip, my breathing tripping out of me as anticipation turned the blood in my veins molten.

His blue eyes were fixed on my face, darting down to my mouth every few seconds. Then his tongue darted out, wetting his own lips. "Fuck, lass," he breathed the words out, releasing me and stepping back. Grayson was shaking his head, staring at me like I was a meal he was starved to eat but wasn't allowed a single taste.

I took a step toward him, and he shook his head.

"Stay on that fucking side of the room, Sloane. I don't know what I'm capable of right now."

The way he was *hungering* for me emboldened me, though. I stepped closer, seeing his eyes widen before his lust overtook him completely. The air felt charged with electricity, prickling along my skin, heightening my nerve endings, which all seemed to be frayed in his presence.

He swallowed, his Adam's apple bobbing roughly. "Last warning, lass." His words, spoken in a low, graveled drawl, made me hesitate. But it was already too late. I'd been captured by his reaction. As if seeing my resolve, he suddenly broke free of his self-imposed atrophy and lunged at me.

A surprised gasp left my lips when he picked me up effortlessly, wrapping my legs around his waist, and pressed my back against the bedroom door. The wood was cold against my heated skin, but I forgot all about that when Grayson crushed his lips to mine.

Those nerve endings of mine that had been heightened were now sparkling with barely repressed desire.

Desire for my fucking captor.

His tongue was an insistent stroke against the seam of my lips, pressing me, coercing me into letting him inside. I opened for him, shuddering when his tongue swept into my mouth, tasting me everywhere. Exploring me. I gave myself over to his kiss at that point, tasting sandalwood and leather on his lips.

Tangling his hands into my hair, he tilted my head to one side, deepening the kiss. When he nipped my bottom lip, I shuddered. When he sucked on it, I melted more deeply into his hold. My nipples pearled into unbearably hard peaks, and I knew he could feel them through the flimsy material of my camisole pressed against his chest.

With an animalistic snarl, he pressed me tightly against the door to free one of his hands. He stroked over one of my breasts, thumbing the distended nipple before running his fingers over my ribs, along my bared thighs, then back again. He fisted my hair. Kissed my throat. Teased my sensitive flesh without hesitation of rebuke.

It was as if he were blind and wanted to learn how I looked by touch alone.

Beneath my ass, his hips rolled, his hardened flesh meeting my softness and making me gasp. His mouth swallowed down the sound, devouring it hungrily. He broke the kiss, pulling back a fraction, so we were staring at each other from only inches away. We were both breathless. Panting. Turned-on as fuck.

"Grayson," I managed to say, the word barely sounding like it had come from my lips. "What about Fi—"

He stopped me from speaking the clan boss's name. With a fierceness in his blazing eyes, he told me, "I'm already going to hell for this, lass. At least let me enjoy the ride down."

He captured my jaw, tilting my head to the side and up so he could have better access to my throat. Then he tongued my pulse as it thumped impatiently, his teeth grazing along my skin. Then, with a snarl in his throat, he hooked his arms around my thighs and walked us to the edge of the bed.

He placed me on the mattress and dropped to his knees, pushing between my thighs. He tore the camisole top from my body, breaking the thin straps easily, and bared me to him. I didn't have the time to be self-conscious because he was already leaning forward, capturing one nipple in his mouth while his hand palmed the other breast. He sucked and pulled. Squeezed and pinched. All the sensations left me breathless.

Ragged.

Undone.

Darting out his tongue, he teased my aching flesh until I tugged at his hair, begging him to put me out of my misery.

"Touch me." I moaned. "Grayson. *Please*. Touch me."

With rough hands, he split my thighs wider to get around his broad frame and shoved the edge of my silky camisole shorts to the side. His blunt fingers slid past my panties, and I let out a gasp.

"You already wet for me, lass?" he rasped, still stroking into me.

Rolling my bottom lip into my mouth, I thrashed. Writhed.

Grayson fixed his stare on my pussy, on the dip of his fingers. "You want my mouth here?" He flashed a wicked grin. "Of course, you do. You're already dripping."

Bringing his hand up, he showed me how I coated his fingers.

"Open that pretty mouth, Sloane, and taste."

Parting my lips, I sucked his fingers into my mouth, swirling my tongue around the digits. He pulled back and pushed his fingers inside my pussy once more, pumping until I had to grip his wrist.

"Please, Grayson. Please."

Pump in.

Pump out.

"What do you want, lass? You want my mouth on your cunt? You want me to taste you?"

God help me, that was exactly what I wanted. "Yesss." The word was drawn out on a moan.

He chuckled darkly. "Soon," he replied, sliding his fingers back inside me. "I was going to take your pussy, but I want to feel you come on my fingers first. I want to know what that squeeze feels like."

My spine bowed, my arching back pressing my breasts closer to his face. He sucked one nipple into his mouth, lashing it with his tongue—driving my need higher.

Rasping breaths.

Stifled moans.

Bitten off gasps.

Wet sucking.

The sounds we were both making were an auditory eroticism.

Still, his fingers didn't stop sliding into me. Pumping. Curling over that sensitive spot inside me that silently begged for his touch. Sweat sheened my body, my core body temperature sky-rocketing under his skilled hands.

Grayson's hard voice drew me from my pleasure. "Look at me."

My eyes didn't want to open, but I forced them to focus on his face. I was perversely pleased to see that sweat spotted his brow too. His jaw was tight, his sensuous mouth bracketed with concentration. His eyes, however, were half-lidded and glittering with wildfire.

"Look at me while I make you come."

Mutely, I nodded, a shiver wracking my whole body as his plunging fingers brought me right to the edge of release. Then, using his thumb, he began to circle my clit. Once. Twice. On the third revolution, I came undone. My orgasm washed over me like a scorching wave of pleasure, dragging me under. The force of it was so great that my eyes fluttered shut but peeled open again when Grayson growled.

"Eyes. On. Me," he commanded, hyper-focused on my face.

What I saw there was pure lust.

Raw.

Savage.

Desperate.

Everything about this prolonged my orgasm until I was finally boneless and panting against the comforter.

He was still stroking into me, wringing little aftershocks of pleasure from my body until I had to beg him to stop. Withdrawing from my body, he drew his fingers into his mouth and tasted me, licking, savoring. When he was done, he pinned me with his icy-blue eyes and murmured one word.

"Honey."

II
GRAYSON

I WAS SO FUCKING ON EDGE.

Orgasm denial was grand, but not when it involved my own denied release. I only had myself to blame for that, though. I had no doubt Sloane would've let me slide right into her tight body and fuck her into oblivion. And now that I knew what she felt like when she came? I was a fucking desperate man to feel that squeeze on my cock.

"Are you ready?"

I blinked at Finnan, who had his arms hanging over the top rope of the sparring ring. I stood up, re-adjusting my semi-hard cock in my shorts. Hauling myself up the stairs, I ducked under the rope as Finnan held it for me and stepped onto the canvas. The floor was springy as I jumped up and down a few times to get the blood to move from my cock to other parts of my body.

If only I could forget the way she tasted.

If only I could stop hearing those desperate little mewls she made down low in her throat as she came.

If only I could stop myself from going back for more.

I'd told her that she was playing a dangerous game, but I was the one who needed the warning. I was the one who knew the rules, knew the consequences, but decided to play anyway.

Finnan brought up his gloved hands, holding them out to me to touch. The leather of our gloves had barely brushed before I was swinging, landing a jab to Finnan's face. His head snapped back, and when he looked at me again, there was a trickle of blood on the corner of his mouth. He darted his tongue out and licked it away before fixing me with a maniacal glare.

"You're out for blood today, Kent? I'll be more than happy to oblige."

I grinned at him, daring him to strike. He did, catching me on the side of the ribs before landing an uppercut to my solar plexus. Air became scarce as I doubled over, but I did not risk taking my eyes off Finnan, who had retreated a few steps.

"I know why I'm wound up, but why are you?" he asked, bouncing on his toes. "Got a problem pussy?"

Fuck. I couldn't tell him the truth, but a lie would serve me just as well. With a grunt, I acknowledged his assumption. "Rhapsody is getting a little too familiar."

"Rhapsody," he repeated with a smile. "She's a kinky little cunt. Need Mary to straighten her out?"

I waved away his suggestion with my gloved hand. "No, I can handle it." Moving forward, I engaged him again, our upper bodies locking, heads together. Our breathing turned ragged as punches were exchanged, the cinch only breaking when Finnan managed to wiggle out from my lock.

We circled each other for a few more seconds, trading quick jabs that had no power behind them. Until I clicked Finnan on his shoulder, spinning him off balance and throwing him against the ropes. When he straightened, anger flashed in his green eyes. I'd wordlessly thrown down the gauntlet, and he'd picked it up. Shrugging his shoulders, he came at me again.

I took punches to my stomach, jaw, and cheek but also managed to land a few hits of my own. After another ten minutes of sparring, sweat was pouring off both of us.

Finnan held up his gloved hand and said, "Enough. We have to get to work."

Ripping the Velcro loose from around my wrists, I pulled off my gloves, dropping them to the canvas.

Finnan flicked sweat from his forehead. "There's been another hijacking."

My brows rose. "Another?"

He grunted. "The first shipment from Kavanaugh was supposed to come through last night. The fucking container was empty after we cleared the furniture that had been stacked in front of it."

"Fuck."

"Yeah." Finnan got out of the ring, and after I scooped up my gloves, I followed.

"What does our guy at the port have to say?"

"He said the container wasn't left unattended *at all*."

"Clearly, he's lying if the shit is missing."

"Maybe. The ship refueled in Dublin before coming here, though."

Taking off my hand wraps, I balled them together and dropped them into my awaiting sports bag. "You think the guns were stolen before they'd even arrived in Galway Port?"

Finnan stripped off his shirt. His skin was glistening with sweat as he drew a towel around his neck. "Aye, I do."

"But how could anyone have known the shipment was even there?" Only the upper echelon of the clan was aware of the deal and the shipping schedule.

"Kavanaugh could just be fucking us over."

"True," I conceded, taking off my own shirt and rubbing away the sweat under my arms. "But would he risk his only daughter's life just to fuck with us like that?"

I could tell Finnan didn't want to acknowledge that. We both walked into the changing room and hit the showers.

Over the spray of water, I heard Finnan ask from his cubicle, "Anything else I need to know?"

I tilted my head back into the spray, letting the sweat sluice off me. "Mary told me that Kitty's ex has been sniffing around."

Finnan's eyes turned black. "If he's laid a fucking finger on her…"

If there was one thing the employees of Velvet knew, it was that the Mac Tíre clan would always have their backs.

"As far as I know, he's just coming around on her off days. Asking questions. That sort of stuff. I told Little John to call me if he came in again." I shut off the faucets and snagged the towel hanging over the door. After drying my face, I wrapped it around my waist and unlocked the door. Finnan was already getting changed, his bag sitting on the long bench.

"How do you like my fiancée?" he asked suddenly, making me jerk my head around to look at him.

My heart was in my mouth as I asked, "What?"

"Sloane Kavanaugh. What do you think of her?"

Fuck. Fuck. *Fuck*. Did he suspect that I'd touched her? Clearing my throat, I gave myself a mental fucking pep talk to stay cool. Rummaging through my bag, I pulled out a pair of boxer briefs and stepped into them, rearranging my semi-hard dick that had perked up at the mention of Sloane. Taking a seat, I slid my legs into my jeans and formulated my answer.

She tasted of honey, just like I knew she would? No.

Her mouth is made for fucking? No.

The sounds she makes when she comes made my dick twitch? Fuck, no.

"She's fucking demanding," I settled on.

"She's a princess. She's used to Daddy handing everything to her on a silver platter. I'll make sure that mentality is gone before too long."

With jerking movements, I got out my shirt and slid it over my head, drawing the fabric down my torso. Knowing Finnan, he was going to have to break Sloane's spirit to get her to become the meek, quiet wife he wanted. I wondered if he was aware of how difficult she was going to make that for him?

"Where do you want me to drop you?" I asked when I was sure my voice wouldn't betray my murderous intent. When he didn't answer, I glanced over at him to find him staring at me. It was like he'd seen straight through my lie.

"Velvet. I need to have a little stress relief before we meet with Doyle this afternoon."

I turned back before he could see my expression. Tucking my dirty clothes back into my bag, I paused when my phone started to ring from the inside pocket.

"Little John?"

"Kitty's ex is here."

I glanced at Finnan. "Thanks. I'm on my way."

FIFTEEN MINUTES LATER, FINNAN AND I WALKED into Velvet. Delux saw the boss and took him by the hand, leading him away to one of the private rooms.

Little John sidled up beside me, too quiet for a man his size. "The skinny lad sitting off to one side of the stage. Looks like a weasel."

"That's offensive to weasels, Little John," I drawled back, cracking my knuckles. Stalking forward, I approached the guy's table. He clearly had no sense of self-preservation because he didn't even look up. A man at another table shifted uncomfortably in his seat before getting up and relocating across the other side of the room.

"You Kitty's ex?" I asked.

The guy finally looked up at me. He took a moment to size me up, then returned his attention to my face. "Yeah. What's it to you, gobshite?"

I let him see the malice in my smile for a brief second

before taking him by the back of the shirt and hauling him behind the table. He dangled a few inches off the floor, his legs kicking.

"Put me down!" he yelled, arms pinwheeling to throw me off balance.

With that same smile still in place, I released his shirt. He hit the table as he fell, the beer he'd been nursing sloshing all over him as the table tipped. He was on his feet a moment later, swinging. I leaned back, letting his fist sail straight by me before cracking him in the jaw. He spun like a top and collapsed onto the floor.

Reaching down, I hauled him up by the back of his shirt and marched him into the staff corridor, then out the back door. I was vaguely aware of Little John following me.

Throwing the fucker against the brick wall, I watched him land in a heap on the gritty ground. Like before, he came up swinging.

"Are you a fucking eejit?" I barked, slamming my fist into his stomach. On his way down, I asked quietly into his ear, "Do you not know that Kitty is under our protection?"

From under the dark mop of hair, he seethed. "Are you her new lover. I was told she had one."

To be sure I'd heard him correctly, I glanced over at Little John. "Does this gobshite not know who I am?"

The big guy shrugged, folding his hands in front of his hips in the classic bodyguard stance.

"Un-fucking-believable." I hauled him up once more, holding him by the shoulder so I could get a good look at his face. *What the fuck did Kitty see in this guy?* "You're going to listen to me, and listen good. You are not to come around here anymore. Kitty knows you're slinking around when she's not working, and that shite ends today. Right now."

"Fuck you," he spat out, defiance gleaming in his eyes. He rose to his feet, his legs a little shaky. "Kitty belongs to me."

"Kitty is a grown-ass woman who can decide who she wants in her life. Unfortunately, you don't seem to be able to grasp this concept, so I'm going to make sure you get it."

Something silver flashed down near his side, and I swore. The bastard had a knife.

His eyes shifted from me to Little John, then back to me. "I won't go down like this."

"Like what?" I asked, pulling my Glock, leveling it at his head, and pulling the trigger.

Brain matter spattered like a bloody firework on the bricks behind him, his body slumping to the ground. With the back of my hand, I wiped away the blood that had been flung onto my face and neck, sneering at it.

Behind me, and without being asked, Little John radioed one of the other guys for help to clean up the body.

Re-holstering my gun at the small of my back, I turned around and met his eyes. "Thanks for the phone call, Little John."

His black eyes gravitated toward the mass of meat against the wall before swinging back to my face. "Nobody will miss the piece of shit."

Nodding, I stepped past him and opened the door. One of the other security guards was already walking down the hallway, and I turned into one of the bathrooms to clean up. Blood covered one side of my face. Blow-back was a bitch. Wetting a wad of paper towels, I rubbed the blood and gray matter from my face, pitching the bloody, sodden mess into the trash can on my way out, knowing Little John would deal with it.

With adrenaline still coursing through me, my dick was as hard as a steel pipe, and there was only one place I wanted to be.

12

SLOANE

WITH ONE LEG TUCKED UP UNDER ME AND A PLATE of toast balanced on the mattress beside me, I'd replayed the way Grayson had touched me this morning over and over as I showered and changed into a shirt and panties. I remembered every single nuance, every sound. The way his muscles were firm and unyielding under my hands. His sandalwood scent. The way my breathy moans had sounded so wanton.

Christ, my panties were damp again just from the memory of having his fingers inside me. I could only imagine how amazing having his cock filling me would feel. Setting the empty plate onto the side table, I laid back in the mountain of pillows and stared at the ceiling, my imagination beginning to sprint away from me.

I shouldn't be lusting after Grayson.

I should be trying to escape from him at every turn.

But the way he'd touched me? My nipples pebbled at the fleeting thought, and I squirmed, pressing my thighs together to relieve the ache that hadn't really stopped since he'd left.

Even though my last orgasm was only a few hours old, that throbbing need was back again, and I suspected only Grayson could quench it.

"Stockholm Syndrome," I whispered to myself. "What *the fuck* are you doing, Sloane?"

The pep talk didn't help me, though. If anything, it made Grayson clearer in my mind. And as I snaked my hand down my stomach and under the waistband of my panties, my fingers slid through the slickness that was already pooling. I couldn't believe I was so turned on by the mere thought of a man, but the evidence couldn't be denied.

Rubbing my clit, I shut my eyes and pictured Grayson's fingers there, driving me relentlessly into mind-blowing pleasure. His rough touch would send me tumbling over the edge, but it would be his thorough kisses that would keep me grounded. His mouth wouldn't ask—it would take— demanding things from me that I shouldn't be giving.

Impatient with how restricted the movement was, I shimmied from my panties, leaving me naked from the waist down. Sliding against my wet heat, my hips began to roll against the feel of my fingers, my head thrashing from one side to the other on the pillow. I inhaled sharply, and I could've sworn I smelled sandalwood. My imagination had always been good, but it had never involved smells before. I increased speed as my orgasm loomed over me, threatening to crash and take away all my senses.

"Jesus *Christ.*"

My eyes cracked open a little, then widened when I found Grayson standing in the doorway to my bedroom. I scrambled up, back pressing against the headboard. His eyes had darkened with unbridled lust, his jaw clenched, his body coiled tight like a spring.

"W-what are you doing here?"

Menace swirling around him, he stepped into my room and shut the door. Stalking forward, he stopped at the footboard, leaned over, and gripped my ankle. With one strong tug, he yanked me down the bed. My shirt rucked up my back, exposing my stomach and the underside of my breasts.

With one arm hooked around my thigh, he pushed the other leg wide so I was completely exposed to him. His dark-as-sin eyes drifted from my face to my breasts to my pussy. He thumbed at my clit, making my back arch gracefully off the bed.

"You better have been thinking of me while you were touching yourself," he said in a voice that sounded as if it had been dragged through glass. "Because if you weren't, I'd have to go and kill the bastard you *were* thinking about. Tell me who's mouth, tongue, and cock you were imagining as you touched yourself."

"Yours." It was a whisper. A lament. Because I was grieving my self-control. Where the fuck did it go when this man was involved?

I whimpered when I felt his hot breath feather across the inside of my thigh a second before he licked through my pussy. Pleasure sparked through me, making my breath catch and goose bumps break out on my body.

He planted an open-mouthed kiss against my opening, his tongue stroking through my flesh on a slow sweep. My spine bowed, sending my shoulders and upper back into the mattress while my hips lifted. Grayson held me in place, his fingers strong and sure around my thigh and knee, where he held me open to feast.

And I was a feast for him.

He lapped at me. Sucked. Bit. Punished with lashes of his tongue. Growls of pleasure pumped out of him, the sounds so primal they made my bones quake with need.

Sliding one finger, then another, into my pussy, my inner walls clamped down immediately, sending a wave of pleasurable anticipation through my blood. Grayson swept his tongue through my folds, then used the tip to flick rhythmically against my clit.

"Fuck, Grayson," I gasped, feeling the first hints of my orgasm. "Do that again."

He did.

And my orgasm answered his touch. My inner muscles tightened, and I jerked away, flexing my hips upward, surrendering to my pleasure.

Grayson growled and gripped my body tighter, holding me against his face as I came so hard that I felt like I wasn't in my body for a second. My mouth opened in a scream, and he had the good sense to smother the noise with his hand before it could reach a crescendo.

"The guards are still outside," he hissed, licking through me and humming his satisfaction. "And I haven't had enough of your honey yet."

Latching onto my clit, he sucked hard, sending a shower

of aftershocks through my body. The secondary orgasm washed over me gently, though. Instead of the fierce crash like the first, this one glided over me, prolonged by the slow, languid laps of Grayson's tongue.

"Enough!" I gasped. "Enough, Grayson." I shoved at him, my over-sensitized flesh not recognizing the pleasure anymore.

He pulled away, running his tongue across his top lip. "You taste better than I imagined you would… better than every single one of my fantasies."

Getting to his feet, he pulled a phone from his pocket and glanced at the screen.

When he turned his head, I noticed there was blood on the side of his neck. I pointed at the offending spot. "You have blood on you."

He touched where I was pointing, then looked at me. And I could've sworn I saw regret flicker in his blue gaze before he went back to giving me a hard stare. "I have to go."

He had to go? After giving me two orgasms, he *had to go*? "What?"

"Finnan needs me."

"So, what, you thought you'd come back here, eat me out, then leave?" I glared at his painfully obvious erection. "You're giving yourself blue balls."

He glanced down at the offending protrusion in his jeans, then back to me. "I've had blue balls since the day I first saw you, lass."

I was left gaping, unable to come up with something to say to that. "Well, what am I supposed to do now? Just sit around and wait for Finnan to *summon* me? Wait for you to come back and participate in some more deviant behavior?"

He leveled me with a heated stare. "What should you do? You should remember the feel of my tongue in your pussy so when you pleasure yourself to the memory... *again*..." he smirked, "... you'll be wet and ready." His voice had taken on a hard edge that I feared I would always associate with sex.

Good, hard, rough sex.

With him.

When he reached the door, he stopped and spoke over his shoulder, "Finnan wants you to meet him for dinner later."

"Just with him?"

"No. With some of the clan."

"He wants to show me off," I surmised.

His jaw flexed for a moment. "I'll be back at six to pick you up."

Then he was gone.

13

GRAYSON

IT TOOK EVERYTHING I HAD IN ME NOT TO TURN around and walk back into her bedroom. Walking in to find her masturbating to thoughts of me had nearly brought me to my knees. Sloane was utter perfection, and I vowed to learn every secret her body held.

I had never meant for her to see the blood, though. For the first time in my life, I felt ashamed that she had to see it. Logically, that thinking was fucked up. She knew who her father was. She knew that this life was messy, but I didn't want her to see me like that for some reason.

I shut the apartment door behind me, running a hand through my hair as I did. Fuck. I was wound so fucking tight, but I could still taste her on my tongue. Shoving my hand into the pocket of my jeans, I pulled out my phone once more and looked at the screen.

Two missed calls from Fallon and a text.

Four missed calls from Finnan.

I shot Finnan a text telling him I was on my way, then called Fallon.

"Fallon, what's up?" I asked as soon as she answered.

"Why would anything be up?" she asked.

"Because I saw you this morning at home and things were fine."

"I just called to see if you were with Sloane."

Pointlessly and without reason, I bristled. I forced myself to breathe before saying, "Why would I be with Sloane?"

"Ah, because she's gorgeous, and I thought you were tapping that."

I gritted my teeth. "I'm not tapping that. She's Finnan's fiancée, for fuck's sake." Despite that, Sloane and I were both on a freight train with broken brakes. Eventually, we would collide—the only question was *when*?

I knew it was ridiculous giving into my stupid fucking impulses, but from the first moment I'd seen her, she'd held *me* captive rather than the other way around.

"What do you want?"

"Is Sloane around?"

"I just left her apartment. Why?"

"I wanted to take her shopping then go out for lunch. Maybe show her the sights."

I rubbed at my eyes. "I can't let her go anywhere unprotected. Plus, Finnan needs me today."

"So, send someone with her."

I couldn't tell her that I didn't trust anyone else with her care. "Who the hell would want to trail around with you and Sloane?"

"How about Torin? All he does is drive you around, right?"

"Yeah," I replied slowly, wondering where the hell she was going with this.

"How about he drops you off to do whatever it is you do with Finnan, and he comes with us."

My instinct was to say *hell no* to the proposition, but before the words could form, I stopped. I thought about it. My men already knew that I'd spent more time than necessary with her this morning—and just now—and that I'd spent even more the night before. If I refused to let someone watch her today, it would give them more reason to talk.

Even though it killed me, I gritted out a "Fine."

Fallon let out a little whoop of excitement. "Want Torin to bring her to me, or should we meet somewhere?"

"Meet somewhere," I replied. "I'll go and ask Sloane now."

"Just give her your phone," Fallon said.

My brows rose. "Why?"

"I'll sell the idea to her better than you can."

I would do just about anything for my sister, but she knew how far to fucking push me. Turning on my heel, I marched back to the apartment door and opened it. Sloane was in the kitchen, taking a sip of what smelled like coffee from a white porcelain mug. She was still wearing a white t-shirt that showed the shadow of her dusty pink nipples and a pair of black lace panties, but I averted my eyes so I could focus. With my jaw tight, I thrust my phone at her.

With a puzzled expression, she took it and then put it to her ear. Whatever my sister said to her made a small smile appear on her face.

"Sure. I'd love that," Sloane replied. "When?... Okay. Great. See you then."

When the call was over, Sloane handed back the phone.

"What time did Fallon want to meet?"

"In an hour."

Finnan could wait. I took the coffee cup from her hand and waved her off. "I'll wait for you."

AN HOUR LATER, TORIN PULLED THE ROVER TO A STOP outside a café in town and put the car into park. Fallon was waiting on the curb, practically vibrating with excitement. I got out of the car, circling the back and opening Sloane's door.

The two women greeted each other with a hug while I slammed the door shut. Turning to Torin, I gave him *the look*. The look that said I'd have his balls on a platter if he fucked this up and either Sloane or Fallon got hurt.

"They're safe with me, Grayson," he said, trying to reassure me. It was too fucking bad that the only way I'd be reassured was if I was going with the pair. But Finnan was waiting for me, so I had to relinquish control this time.

"Check in with me every thirty minutes. Get her back by six." I rounded the hood of the car and got into the driver's seat, tearing away from the curb, and Sloane, before I could change my mind.

I drove too fast to the warehouse where Finnan had set up his primary offices. Even though it looked like a run-of-the-mill industrial building, there were more security measures in place than a maximum-security prison.

Nodding to the guards on the way through the building, I entered the office and found Finnan behind his desk.

"Where the fuck have you been?" he barked.

"Your bride-to-be can be demanding," I replied, hoping he didn't read into my statement too much. She was demanding, but in a way that I liked.

"She's got a mouth on her, that's for sure." He leaned back in his chair, interlacing his hands and resting them on his stomach. "I hope that fire is an indication of what she's like in bed." He laughed at that, and I joined in because it was better than pulling out my Glock and putting two bullets in his brain.

Sloane wasn't mine...

... but I wanted her to be.

"We should go if you want to make the meet," I said, glad that my voice didn't betray the murderous rage I actually felt.

Finnan rose from his chair, buttoning up his suit jacket as he did. He was the same height as me but not as broad through the shoulders. He'd inherited the clan after the death of his father, so there'd never been a need for him to bulk up the way I had.

"Found out who the rat is yet?" he asked as he passed.

Christ, it had only been five hours since I'd last seen him. "No."

Finnan's jaw muscle ticked. "Then what the fuck have you been doing today?"

I bit my tongue. "Cleaning house."

"Found out another shipment got jacked this morning… this time, it was a lorry that turned up empty. That's two shipments in less than a twelve-hour period." He rounded on me, jabbing his finger into my chest as he said, "Find the fucker who's fucking us over and deliver me his *fucking* head on a spike."

For a long minute, we stared at each other from only a few inches apart. I watched as Finnan stowed away his anger methodically—like it was a real effort to gear down after an outburst. When he rolled his shoulders back and straightened the fall of his jacket, he asked in a neutral voice, "Is everything set for today?"

I didn't let him see me breathe out a deep breath. "I have both buyers meeting us ten minutes apart. They'll have to pass each other in the hall and know they're in direct competition for our business."

"Good. There's nothing more I like than messing with these fuckers."

When we got to the main entrance of the warehouse, Finnan hung back and waited for me to precede him. I was the dispensable one here—not him. I tapped the door, letting the guard on the other side know who it was. He opened it, his AR-15 strapped across his chest and held in place down by his side.

"Boss," one of them said as Finnan passed.

I scanned the surrounding buildings even though this was still technically a 'safe' zone. I never relaxed when I was guarding the boss. Reaching around to the small of my back, I gripped the handle of my Glock and started forward.

When we made it to the car, I opened the door and waved

in Finnan.

Once I was in the driver's seat, I shifted the car into gear and peeled away from the building. The roads were slick with rain, the wipers on the Rover picking up speed as I accelerated. We were going to one of the dummy offices the clan owned, always changing the location of meets in case the businessmen we worked with foolishly decided to share insider knowledge with the cops.

Today, we were heading to a corporate building not far from the restaurant where I'd taken Sloane. We were meeting up with two different businessmen who wanted in on our freighting business. The kicker was that each of the men vying for a piece of our pie were rivals, and Finnan was banking on the fact that the two men would try to outbid one another if they knew their competition was interested.

We arrived first, and Finnan took a seat at the head of a long table inside the boardroom. I stood behind him, my hands clasped in front of my hips.

"It's imperative that we squeeze as much from these assholes as we can," Finnan said, casually brushing lint from the sleeve of his suit jacket.

"Yes, sir."

"We don't get this deal, then we don't have the funding we need to expand our trade operations. If it doesn't happen here, you need to make it happen out there."

What he didn't need to say was that if shit went sideways tonight, I had his blessing to coerce one of the two men into an understanding—one that would involve the safety and well-being of their families. "Understood."

We didn't have to wait long for the first of our potential

investors to arrive. Sean Doyle entered the boardroom flanked by two men. Dressed in expensive suits, one looked like a lawyer, who wore his disdain for us on his slightly too-feminine face. The other looked like a younger version of Doyle, and I figured it was his son, learning how business was done when you wanted to get into bed with the mob.

That was perhaps the first mistake Sean Doyle had made. He'd shown me how much he valued his son's input, which would make threatening him all the easier.

"Mr. Quinn," he said to Finnan. "This is my son, Cian, and my lawyer, Mr. Byrne."

The younger Doyle, Cian, nodded, and the lawyer offered Finnan his hand. Finnan stared at the offered appendage before his gaze flickered back to Doyle Senior.

"Take a seat, Doyle. Let's get down to it."

The elder Doyle blinked at him before sitting in the seat Finnan had gestured to. The lawyer sat beside him, but his son remained on his feet.

"You understand the purpose of this meeting. You know what's for sale." Finnan waited for his nod of understanding before continuing, "For a twenty percent stake in our freighting business, you have to submit your best offer."

Doyle reached into his inner suit jacket pocket, and I unhooked my hands and pulled my Glock into view. It was a non-verbal warning that he had to tread extremely carefully. Doyle's eyes widened slightly, and his son eased back a step.

Reaching out, Byrne touched Doyle on the forearm, stopping him from pulling whatever it was from his pocket.

"Mr. Quinn, we understand what's at stake. You need investors. My client needs reassurance that his bid for the twenty percent will guarantee not just a monetary return but also access to the freighting routes for his own personal use."

From where I was standing, I couldn't see Finnan's reaction to that, but he made a *continue* gesture with his hand.

Byrne nodded, and Doyle pulled out a crisp, white envelope to slide across the table to Finnan.

Keeping my Glock out, I reached out to take the offer, passing it to my boss, who slid his finger under the flap and opened the envelope. He pulled out a piece of paper no bigger than the size of a business card.

The figure written on the back was done in a cursive script that looked like it belonged somewhere in the eighteen hundreds. I guessed private education not only got you more wealth but more useless skills that could never really be used in real life. Like fucking calligraphy.

Like buying into a business that dealt with more illegal shit than most people would be comfortable with.

The figure on the card said five-hundred thousand.

It was a fair offer—in line with what Finnan was thinking, but intimidation could you get him a hell of a lot more.

"So, what say you, Mr. Quinn?" Byrne demanded bluntly.

With an ominous *thud*, I placed my Glock down on the table, pointing the barrel in Byrne's direction. The lawyer's wide-eyed gaze flickered from the gun to me. "Are you threatening me?" he demanded.

"Aye, I am."

"We're here trying to make a deal, and you think that pointing a gun in my and my client's direction will make us, what? Offer more?"

"That's the idea, aye."

His lips twisted. "You're a bunch of thugs."

My lips curled up in the corner. "We're the Mac Tíre Clan. Of course, we're thugs."

He sputtered, "This is a legal deal."

"Aye, it is," I replied. I jerked my chin in old man Doyle's direction. "And he wants in. Badly. So, why don't you let *him* talk?"

Byrne returned his attention to Doyle Senior. "Sir, I must insist that you reconsider getting into business with these men. This one…" he gestured to me, "… is going to threaten you into offering more."

"I was going to threaten him regardless of his offer," I said.

Byrne looked outraged all over again but shut his mouth when Doyle said, "He has what we need, Liam." His voice was hard. "And I refuse to let that Egyptian asshole Ahmed Hassan get the better of me again!" He slammed his hand onto the desk when he hissed out his adversary's name. There really was nothing like a rivalry to make a man lose his senses.

Finnan lifted his fingers, silencing me. "Excuse my associate here. He's more in the business of cracking skulls than talking business." He let out a sigh. "In answer to your question, Mr. Byrne," Finnan began. "The deal is barely within the limits of acceptable offers. But I think you can do better."

"I don't understand, Mr. Quinn. I came here with an offer. You either accept it or don't."

"We have two parties interested in this stake of our business… you and one other. After I've received the bid from the other potential investor, you will be able to submit one more bid."

"Who is the other interested party?" Doyle Junior asked in a small voice.

The other man seemed to shrink away when Finnan's eyes locked on his face. "That's confidential, *bhuachaill*."

The junior Doyle's face puckered at the use of the Gaelic word for 'boy.' Finnan, though, had done it on purpose to let Doyle know that we were well aware of what he was attempting to do.

Finnan rose from his chair, buttoning up his suit jacket as he did. "Someone will be in touch in the next day or two."

"Why bother coming down here at all if there's no negotiation?" Byrne asked, seemingly recovered from his little outburst.

"Why?" Finnan asked. "Because when I make a deal with someone, I want to look in their eyes and see that they're worthy." He held out his arm to the door. "Now, if you don't mind, the other interested party will be here shortly."

Doyle and Byrne rose from their chairs, their heads together while they discussed how fucked they were.

"Doyle," Ahmed Hassan said from the doorway, making Sean Doyle's head jerk up like it was attached to a string. Hassan's arms were folded as he wore a smug look on his face. "Trying to undercut me again? Didn't you learn from the last time you tried?"

"Hassan?" Doyle sputtered. He turned to Finnan. "This is the other interested party?"

Finnan remained quiet, letting the fireworks go off around him.

"Going to withdraw your offer now, are you, Doyle?" There was no shadow of a foreign accent from Hassan, even though he'd been born in Egypt.

Doyle didn't dignify that with an answer. He brushed past the other man, his lawyer following close behind. Cian Doyle was the last through the door, but I noticed he lingered as he passed Hassan, and from my angle, I saw the brush of their fingers.

Into Finnan's ear, I whispered, "Cian Doyle and Ahmed Hassan are fucking each other."

Finnan nodded to tell me he'd heard.

"Mr. Hassan, please sit," Finnan said, gesturing to the seat Doyle had vacated.

Ahmed came into the room without a lawyer or entourage. Dressed in a well-cut designer suit, he took a seat effortlessly, resting one ankle on the opposite knee. His arrogant expression faltered a little when he saw the Glock still sitting naked on the desktop.

Without prompting, he reached into the inside pocket of his jacket and pulled out an envelope, then slid it over to me. I already liked this guy better than that old fuck, Doyle.

My boss looked inside the envelope, and I caught sight of the figure written on a piece of card. Seven-hundred and fifty thousand Euros.

Finnan folded back the envelope and placed it on the table. "Generous offer."

"I can see what Doyle can't," Hassan replied in a confident tone, never taking his eyes from Finnan's face. Even though

I was the bigger threat, he knew who was top dog here.

"And what's that?"

"Potential. Growth. A scale of which is impossible anywhere else. And I want to be a part of it."

"It's a good offer."

Hassan tipped his head back and laughed. "It's an exceptional offer. Your business has a net worth of two point eight million euros. Twenty percent of that is five-hundred and sixty thousand."

"So why offer me more than it's worth?"

The other man sat forward in his seat, resting his forearms on his knees and clasping his hands. "Because I can see the value that Doyle can't. I want the share. I want it so much that I'll pay over the twenty percent it's worth because you are a businessman, Mr. Quinn, and you know you cannot walk away from this."

The men stared at each other for a long while before Finnan said, "How much do you want to fuck up this deal with Doyle?"

Ahmed's smile wilted a little, but he quickly covered the reaction with an elegant shrug. "It would bring me great pleasure."

Finnan actually laughed at that. "All right, Mr. Hassan, I'll call you in the next twenty-four hours with my answer."

The other man nodded and left the office.

Then Finnan turned to me. "The winning bid is clear. Hassan is a straight shooter. He doesn't bring lawyers in to try and intimidate. He's got brass balls to offer three-quarters of a million for a fraction of a share in our business. If Doyle managed to up his bid to be the slightest bit competitive, we'd have to deal with him and his pencil-dick lawyer."

"Hassan would be my choice."

Finnan rose from his seat once more, buttoning his jacket. "I still want you to fuck with Doyle and see how much we can get out of him." He glanced at his watch. "I need to attend to some business before the dinner tonight. Trigger will drive me. Make sure Sloane wears a dress. Makeup. Heels. I need her to impress."

And with that, he left.

I ran a hand through my hair, realizing it had been more than an hour and a half since I'd entrusted Torin with Sloane, and there hadn't been one text or call in that time. I pulled out my phone, ready to tear him a new one, when the device began to ring.

"How are they?" I demanded.

"Fine. They stayed at the café for a while."

"They're not there now?"

"No. They wanted to go lingerie shopping."

My hearing sparked out a little before I said, "Did you say *lingerie?*"

"Yeah. Fallon mentioned something about needing new panties or some shite."

The *fuck?*

"Sloane went in after her."

My free hand curled into a fist on instinct, but I released it with a deep breath. "Which store?"

14

SLOANE

"BLACK OR RED?" I ASKED FALLON, HOLDING UP the two different garter belts I'd found—not that we were in this store for me. Fallon had been the one to step inside first, but once I caught sight of all the beautiful lingerie sets, I was hooked.

"Hmm?" Fallon was distracted by the panties when she glanced up. "What?"

"Black or red?" I repeated.

One garter was a wide panel of black lace that covered all the way up to my waist, and the other was more of a classic style that sat low on the hips and was made from a thicker red lace.

"I'd have to see them on to decide," Fallon replied.

I lowered my arms. "Seriously?"

She shrugged. Smiled. Made a little shooing motion with her hands. "Go."

I retreated into the fitting room at the back of the lingerie shop and drew the curtain across. We'd been in the store for only a few minutes, leaving Torin outside to keep watch. When we'd walked in, our babysitter had spoken to the owner of the store, then offered her a stack of bills. She promptly locked the door after him and told us we had free rein and that nobody would disturb us.

I was used to my father getting people to do what he wanted, but the Irish sure had a way about them that my father could never have replicated.

"You know this whole process is pointless, don't you? I don't have my purse, let alone any bank cards or cash to spend."

"Sloane, please," Fallon began—like this was an old argument we were having again. "This purchase is on my brother."

I narrowed my eyes even though she couldn't see it. I hoped she heard the distrust in my voice when I said, "And *how* exactly is Grayson paying for this when he's not here?"

The other woman snorted. "I have his card."

I stuck my head out of the curtain, finding the other woman smiling. "Have it, how? Did he give it to you?"

Her grin only grew wider. "Not exactly, but he would want you to buy yourself something nice. After all, you are being held here against your will."

That was a diplomatic way to put it.

Stripping out of my skinny jeans, I tried on the first garter, leaving my pale pink lace panties in place. The red looked too contrasting against the pink, but the fabric was soft and hugged my body well enough.

I was going to call Fallon over to get her opinion, but I could hear her talking to the owner of the store, so I didn't bother. Unhooking the red garter belt, I placed it carefully on the plush velvet chair in the corner of the fitting room, then picked up the black garter. The lace panel had a slight stretch to it, and as I pulled it into place and secured it, I turned around to look at myself in the mirror. Bunching up my sweater, I got a better understanding of how the lingerie sat.

It covered me from mid-waist down to the tops of my thighs. It was more modest than I initially thought, but somehow that made it sexier. Like stripping was more pleasurable for the viewer when there was less skin to see in the beginning.

I fingered the lace at my waist, tipping my head from one side to the other, and I tried to decide whether I really liked it enough to buy it. Or should I say *Grayson* would buy it. It was his money I was spending, after all.

Did I need a new garter belt? No, probably not. I had no intention of letting Finnan get his hands on me dressed like this. If he wanted to fuck me, he had to do it while I was in period panties and a training bra.

My eyes darted up when the velvet curtains parted unexpectantly, and the man who had been haunting my thoughts since he left abruptly this morning filled the space.

"Grayson?"

Beyond the dressing room, the front door of the lingerie shop opened and closed. I strained to hear Fallon, but it was quiet except for my racing pulse and Grayson's hard breathing.

"Where have they gone?"

His voice was like gravel when he spoke. "Away." His long fingers skimmed down to my ass, then between my legs. He rubbed between my thighs, forcing me to widen my stance. Leaning down, he bit the side of my neck, making me draw in a surprised gasp.

He rolled his tongue against the bite, soothing away the sting he had caused. His other hand traveled under my sweater to cup one breast, pulling away the light pink lace cup that matched my panties. My nipples instantly hardened for him, and he growled against my neck.

Through half-lidded eyes, I watched us in the mirror. Me in a garter belt and panties, with my sweater up to my chest and my cheeks, flushed with color. And Grayson stood behind me like a god. Tall. Broad through the shoulders. His hair brushed against my cheek as he sucked lightly on my collarbone.

An impatient snarl bubbled up between us, and he jerked back, taking the hem of my sweater and tugging it off my body.

I shivered.

His now darker blue eyes met mine in the mirror. "I'm going to make you come so hard you won't be able to see straight. Hands on the mirror in front of you."

I placed my palms against the cool surface and braced myself for what was to come. Grayson's big palm brushed my hair from the side of my face. His breath was hot as he whispered exactly what he intended to do to me into my ear.

"I'm going to eat your pussy again. I *need* to have that taste on my tongue. While I lick and suck at you, I'll slide two fingers inside and pump them in and out. I'll make you so wet for me. Tell me you want that too, baby," he said against the skin of my neck. He licked my pulse point, making my heart leap in my chest.

He bit me this time, taking the chords of my neck in between his teeth and applying just enough pleasure that I turned to liquid in his arms. My hands came off the mirror as I slumped backward, and it was only Grayson's strong arms banded around me that kept me upright. He pressed me forward, urging me to assume that same position as before. When he was sure I would stay there, he tore my panties from my hips but left the black garter belt in place.

His hips surged forward, and I felt his hard cock pressing between my ass cheeks. A delicious ache formed between my legs, and—as if sensing it—Grayson slid his fingers between my folds to rub it away.

"Jesus, you're wet, lass," he moaned against my shoulder.

I writhed against his body, undulating against him.

Grayson rubbed my clit, circling the sensitive bud until I was bucking against him, moaning his name, arching my back, and rolling my hips to try and get more friction.

"My greedy girl," he said with a masculine chuckle. "You want more?"

Drawing my face closer to his, he took my mouth in a bruising kiss while one finger—then another—slid inside my slick channel. The sensation of him filling me sent shocks of pleasure through me. I moaned into his mouth and he swallowed the sound. He pumped his fingers inside me, curling the ends to brush past the most sensitive part of me.

Unexpectedly, I came with a scream.

"That's right, baby, come for me," he said against my mouth before claiming another kiss. When we broke apart, I was panting, feeling every single one of my nerve endings like they'd been set alight and left so he could watch them burn. I glanced in the mirror as he dropped to his knees and wrapped his strong fingers around my thighs—making room for his broad shoulders.

He licked me, and because he was behind me, I could see the flash of his tongue in the mirror's reflection as it lashed against my clit. The erotic scene made that deep pressure begin to build once more, and I was helpless against it.

"I'm coming again," I whispered, my breath fogging up the glass. "Jesus, I'm coming, Grayson. I'm coming."

He grunted, upping the speed of his tongue. I was riding the edge of my orgasm, and when Grayson bit the inside of my thigh, I screamed my release. I came so hard that I did see those stars he promised I'd see.

It was a long minute before my breathing returned to normal and my erratic pulse calmed. Grayson was standing in front of me, his blue eyes raking over my body from head to foot. He rubbed at his glistening mouth, wet from my arousal, and I swallowed hard.

He looked at the time, then glanced back at me, regret in his eyes. Regret at having left me, or regret for coming to me again?

Whatever the reason, I didn't get a chance to ask because he said, "I have to go."

15

GRAYSON

SHE'S SAFE, YOU BASTARD. SHE'S WITH TORIN.

But no matter how many times I said the words to myself, my protective brain told me it was bullshit. The only way I could know she was safe was if she was in my line of sight at all times.

Watching Sloane come had to be my new favorite pastime, but I was a fool to think that this could go on forever. She didn't know I was breaking one of the biggest rules the clan had, and when she found out, I didn't know whether she would keep her mouth shut or sell me out to Finnan.

Rearranging my raging hard-on, I hit the accelerator, sending the Rover hurtling down the M18. The promise I'd made to myself not to fuck her felt like it was starting to feel less and less critical. Feeling her come on my fingers was heaven. Knowing I would never be able to feel her coming on my cock was hell.

I was on a slippery slope—one that would end with me in Sloane's bed at some point.

The main offices for Doyle Enterprises were an hour away in Limerick, giving me plenty of time to think about what the fuck I was doing with her. I thought I'd be content not sinking my cock into her, but with each taste, the more I wanted.

I was obsessed before.

Now, I was addicted.

To her sweet mouth.

To her sharp wit.

To her tight, wet pussy.

I knew we were playing a dangerous game. Shit, I should've been more focused on finding out who the rat was. Another shipment got jacked, and Finnan was on the warpath. We had no idea how our deals were being leaked before they could happen. It was a fucking wonder this deal with Doyle hadn't been cut at the knees either.

Turning up the radio, I tuned out all thoughts of Sloane and focused on getting my job done.

FORTY-EIGHT MINUTES LATER AND INNUMERABLE flashbacks to spreading Sloane wide and tasting her, I pulled up to the curb of the Doyle Enterprises building in Limerick. The office block was the tallest in the city, all tinted glass and steel.

Getting out of the car, I strolled inside, making my way

to the bank of elevators at the rear of the foyer. Just as the door was closing, a young security guard noticed I was there and started toward me. His older counterpart grabbed him by the back of the shirt and hauled him to a stop before he took more than a few steps and whispered something harshly into his ear. The kid looked up at me, the color draining from his face.

The elevator ride was smooth, and when I arrived on the top floor, a sprawling, open-planned office spread out before me. There was a receptionist desk directly opposite the elevator bank, so new arrivals had no choice but to engage.

The woman began to speak before looking up from her computer. "Welcome to Doyle Enterprise. Do you have an appoint—" Her eyes bulged. "Shit." She immediately grabbed the phone, but I slammed my hand on top of hers, stopping her.

I shook my head. "Security won't be able to help you…" My eyes flickered down to her name badge. "Lisa. So, why don't you just let me in to see Mr. Doyle, and I'll be on my way."

She swallowed. "The senior Mr. Doyle isn't here right now. Only his son."

I felt the smile pull at my lips. "I'll speak to him then." Slowly, I lifted my hand from hers so she could dial Cian's office.

Not taking her eyes off me, she licked her lips and said, "Sir, there's a gentleman here to see you. He's… Wait!" She called after me, but I was already on my way down the short hall to find Cian Doyle's office.

Doyle Junior didn't even rise from his chair when he saw me. If anything, he looked resigned, as if he knew this was going to eventually happen.

"Mr. Doyle," I said as I shut the door to the office behind me. "You remember me?"

He nodded. "You're Mr. Quinn's man."

"Right you are," I replied, taking a seat across from his desk. Even though there was at least five feet of barrier between us, he shifted back in his seat, putting even more space there.

"What do you want?"

"I want to talk to you."

His pale blue eyes flittered across the room, never settling on one particular thing. "About what? My father already warned me this would happen... that you would come for me."

Well, now my interest was piqued. "Did he now? What else did he tell you?"

"H-he said you'd try to intimidate me or threaten me into increasing the bid, but you'd be wasting your time if you did."

"Oh?"

His eyes darted around, looking behind me and probably waiting for security to arrive. "Yes. I have no authority to increase the bid. My father is the only one with full controlling power of the company."

I made a show of looking around his office. It was spacious. Lots of soft furnishings. Books on the bookshelf to my left. A huge plate-glass window looking out over the city on my right. Large, powerful desk in front of me. "So, what's all this for?" I gestured to the office. "Show?"

Cian grimaced. "It was my mother's dying wish that I take over the family business. It was a wish my father didn't echo, but he could never deny his wife what she wanted. This was his compromise... the illusion of responsibility." His tone had turned bitter, and I caught a peek behind the professional curtain.

I looked at his left hand as he folded it onto the blotter in front of him, noticing the ring. "How long have you been married?"

He looked down at the gold band, rubbing his thumb along it. "Almost two years."

"And does she or your da know that you're fucking Ahmed Hassan?"

He blinked. "Excuse me?"

"You heard me. Does your da know that you're literally getting fucked up the ass by his biggest rival?" As soon as the question was out of my mouth, it dawned on me. "Wait, does your father hate him *because* he's fucking you up the ass?"

Cian hung his head. "He doesn't know we're in a relationship."

"How long has it been?"

"Three years."

"And where does this rivalry come from?"

"Ahmed attempted to take over another one of my father's companies a few years ago. That's how me and Ahmed met. Ahmed backed out of that deal on account of me, but after my father told him in no uncertain terms what he thought of Egyptian immigrants, Ahmed made it his mission to undercut or outbid him at every turn."

It's almost too easy. I felt the smile curl up the corners of my mouth. "Has anyone else figured it out?"

His eyes met mine. "No."

"Not even your wife?"

"No."

Stretching my legs out under the table, I rested my hands on my stomach and leveled him with a stare. "How much would you be willing to pay to keep this secret quiet?"

He shook his head. "I don't understand. I already told you my father has complete control over business decisions."

"And if I told you the figure Hassan bid? Would that light a fire under your da's arse?"

For the first time, Cian shifted in his seat. "How much did he go over?"

"Probably more than your da would be willing to spend."

"You're going to blackmail him into upping his bid?"

I shook my head. "No. I'm blackmailing *you* into manipulating *him* into upping his bid." I paused, making sure I had his full attention. "To a million Euros."

For a moment, the younger Doyle only blinked as that number resonated in his head. Licking his lips nervously, he asked, "And if I can't make this happen?"

"I tell him about Hassan… him and your lovely wife." I flashed him a smug grin, then rose from my chair, rapping my knuckles on the desk. "I'll expect your father's new bid in the next twenty-four hours."

I walked from the office, wondering when the last time it was that I hadn't had to involve my knuckles or gun to convince people to see things my way.

16

SLOANE

"I DON'T THINK A MAN SHOULD EVER HAVE TO ASK to go down on a woman," Fallon said, flipping through the magazine she had spread out in front of her on my bed. "He should get in there and do it, you know? Make that kitty purr."

I laughed. "Cunnilingus for the win," I agreed. As I said the words, I couldn't help but shiver as I remembered how her brother had done just that.

Grayson had taken what he wanted. And I had enjoyed every moment of it.

"Does my brother ask to go down on you?"

I felt the blush creep up my cheeks. In my most strident voice, I said, "Your brother and I aren't involved."

Her blue-eyed stare was probing, and when she arched a brow—non-verbally calling bullshit on me. "He sent me and Torin away at the lingerie shop, then locked the door.

You two were probably fucking like bunnies back there."

"We were having a private conversation."

"And at the club… he watched you like a hawk."

"He was watching me to make sure I didn't escape." I hedged. Shit. I had to get out of there. "You want more coffee?" I asked, rolling off the edge of the mattress. "Or a saucer of milk for your pussy?"

She groaned. "If milk is a euphemism for a hard dick, I'll take that. It's been too long."

"You're not dating anyone?"

The humor died in Fallon's eyes, and she looked away. "No, I've not had the capacity to date anyone for a couple of years. It's too… soon."

I frowned. I didn't understand what she meant by that, but instead of pushing, I went into the kitchen and fired up the coffee maker in preparation to grind some beans.

I was just about to hit the start button when there was a knock on the door. It was Grayson, and the sight of him made my stomach flip. He was wearing black slacks and a white button-up shirt, the cuffs of which were rolled up to his elbows, showing off his deliciously muscular and veined forearms.

Christ.

He rested his arm porn against the door frame and stared hungrily at me. "Sloane."

Just my name on his lips made my body remember how he'd made me come. Pushing off the jamb, he came into the apartment and shut the door. Advancing toward me, I had no choice but to back up until my spine collided with the wall. Grayson kept coming, crowding me against it and bringing his face closer to mine.

In a husky growl, he told me, "I need another taste of your sweet cunt."

A small mewl escaped my throat, forcing me to press my lips together. His eyes dropped down to my mouth before lifting to my face again.

"I see you want that, too."

I startled when I felt his large hand brush the front of my body, then slide between my thighs until he was cupping my pussy.

He hummed. "It's warm. I bet it's wet too."

Pinning my arms above my head, he held both wrists in his strong grip. My lips parted on a moan, and Grayson took advantage. His mouth met mine in an almost frenzied rush. Tongue. Teeth. Lips. He dominated me with a kiss, a hand between my legs, and restrained arms.

I moaned again when my breasts rubbed against his chest—my nipples abrading and growing hard. The hand he'd had between my legs was repositioned to wrap around my jaw, his fingers tightening. Tilting my head to one side, he deepened the kiss, feeding at my mouth like a starving man.

With a bass growl, he trailed his lips down my throat, nipping, licking, and sucking. He tongued my pulse as it thumped against the side of my neck.

"Grayson," I gasped, flexing my hands in his tight grip. "Fallon's..." I tried to warn him that his sister was just in the other room. "Here."

As if a switch had been thrown, Grayson released me and stepped away. He stared at me with ravenous hunger, his gaze dropping to my mouth and then to my nipples.

"Is that Torin?" Fallon called from the other room—jolting us both out of our lust-induced haze.

Grayson straightened, any sign of his want for me disappearing in an instant. "Why the fuck would it be Torin?" he demanded as Fallon appeared in the kitchen.

I ran an unsteady hand over my mouth, wiping away any evidence of the kiss, and went back to the coffee maker. Like I hadn't just been kissed to within an inch of my life. Jesus.

"Hello, brother," Fallon said cheerfully. "And because he said he'd see me later."

Grayson's brows rose. "I don't want that gobshite around you."

"He's not a gobshite," she defended.

"He knows you're off limits."

She waved his concern off. "What are you doing here, anyway?"

His jaw jumped in irritation. "I have to take you home, and Sloane has to get ready for dinner." He turned his blue eyes to me. "Finnan has asked that you wear a dress and..." he made little air quotes, "... make an effort with your appearance."

"What an arse," Fallon declared as she turned around to grab her bag from the kitchen counter. "I'll see you later, Sloane." Brushing past her brother, she opened the door of the apartment and walked out.

Grayson gave me one final hungry look before following her out and shutting the door behind him.

IT HAD BEEN OVER AN HOUR SINCE GRAYSON HAD BEEN here, yet his sandalwood and leather scent seemed to linger in the air. As I fussed with a curl in the bathroom mirror, I hated that I'd done as Finnan had bid, but I understood it. Being the boss of a clan meant absolute power—whether it be actual power or merely the illusion of it. Tonight was Finnan's night. He was going to show me off like a prize. Tonight was also the night that Grayson and I had to sit there and pretend that he didn't know how I sounded when I came.

Staring at myself in the mirror, I said, "You're a bad-ass bitch, Sloane Kavanaugh. Finnan might be in control here, but you have the right to keep your backbone. You have the right to never back down and not take his shit."

"Who are you talking to?" someone asked from the doorway.

I turned to find Grayson leaning one shoulder casually against the jamb. Dressed in a designer suit, his hair slicked back and a five o'clock shadow on his square jaw, I seriously considered whether he was real. I took my time staring at him. When my eyes finally returned to his face, I found he was taking his fill of me too.

"You wore the other dress I picked for you."

I glanced down at the navy-blue cocktail dress, fingering the soft, frothy fabric of the skirt. "You picked this out?"

"I did."

"What else did you pick out?"

"Everything." The way he said the word made me shiver.

Everything. So dominant. "I wanted easy access to you, which is why I picked short dresses."

I blinked. "Access? Like you knew you'd get into my panties?"

"Yes."

I let out a slow breath as my libido tried to boil over and looked back at my reflection. He stepped up behind me, ghosting his fingers over my shoulders. His blue eyes were serious. "I'm going to find it exceptionally difficult not to shoot every man who stares at you tonight."

"Men won't be staring at me tonight."

He cocked a dark brow. "You obviously don't see what I see then."

"And what is it that you see?"

"A beautiful woman who came thoroughly on my tongue this afternoon in the changing room of a lingerie shop."

A blush hit my cheeks and I cleared my throat.

"Are you wearing the garter belt right now?"

"Yes," I replied in a breathy voice. "And some thigh-highs."

He skimmed his hands up under the skirt of my dress, feeling the lacy edge of the band at the top. He made a *mmm* noise down low in his chest. "I see that."

Grayson gripped my waist and pulled me into his hips. Leaning down, he nipped my neck, then licked away the sting. His erection was firm against my ass, the sensation of all that length and girth making me roll against him.

His fingers tightened. "Jesus, Sloane." He groaned. "You keep doing that, and I'll be shoving you onto your knees."

My mouth dry, I turned around and faced him. "You want me on my knees?"

He stared down into my face, his eyes bouncing between my own. With a warning growl, he said, "You're playing a dangerous game, lass."

"I know," I whispered.

Wrapping a hand around the back of my neck, he pushed me down. I stared at him from my position on the floor, waiting to see what he would do.

With his eyes heavy-lidded, he traced his finger along my cheek, across my bottom lip, and then to the fastening on his slacks. It seemed like he was moving in slow motion as he drew the zipper down.

My eyes dropped when he pulled his cock free from the confines of his black boxer briefs. His erection was long, hard, and veined—the mushroom head blush pink. Starting at the base, he stroked himself twice before threading his fingers through my hair and dragging me closer.

"Open," he murmured.

Parting my lips, I opened my mouth wide for him, enjoying the flash of surprise that crossed his face before he locked down the reaction.

"Tongue out." This time the command was gruffer than the first.

Moistening my mouth, I offered him my tongue, then waited.

"Fuck," he said in a low voice, gripping himself harder. Stroking. When he placed the crown of his cock on my tongue, I swear his eyes rolled back in his head. He seemed to simply absorb the sensation before sliding farther inside.

Jaw tight, he bit out, "Now suck."

Sealing my mouth fully around the shaft, I hollowed out

my cheeks and began to move up and down his length, breathing deeply through my nose. The groan that escaped him sent a shiver through my body and hit me between my legs. God, I was so wet.

As if unable to help himself, he flexed his hips, forcing his cock farther into my mouth. He hit the back of my throat, my gag reflex kicking in and compressing his length.

His fingers tightened in my hair. "Jesus, *fuck*, Sloane. Your mouth…"

I hummed at his praise, but that only served to encourage him. His other hand slid along my jaw, holding firmly while he kept my head immobile and fucked into my mouth.

"Watching the way my dick slides past those pretty painted lips of yours is a fucking sight, lass."

My pussy was throbbing, every shift of the seam against my sensitive flesh torture. I squeezed my thighs together to try and alleviate the ache, but it only served to push my desire higher.

"Touch yourself, Sloane," Grayson commanded, his fierce words ending with a groan. "Now! Touch your cunt."

I snaked a hand between my thighs, finding my panties soaked. Impatient, I shoved them aside and moaned at that first touch. The moan traveled through my throat and straight up Grayson's shaft.

In response, he pulled my hair a little tighter, and the edge between pleasure and pain blurred.

"Christ, lass, you keep making those noises, and I'm going to come."

I pulled back, tapping his hand to let him know to release his hold—to give me the freedom to move. Swirling my tongue around his crown, I took a deep breath, then slid down a little farther, wordlessly telling him to finish inside my mouth. Grayson took the hint and started to pump into me more fiercely than before.

"Close. So close." His words were whispered. Harsh. Desperate.

His thrusts faltered before he barked a harsh "*fuck!*" then came—hard—into the back of my throat. I swallowed him down, savoring the flavor that hit my tongue.

"Are you coming on your fingers, Sloane?" he asked in a strained voice, still thrusting, still coming. "I want to know you're getting off on this, too."

My pace increased, and only two strokes later, I screamed my release around his cock. Pleasure rolled through me until I was deaf to everything except my moans. I rode the waves of euphoria, never wanting to come back down.

Grayson had pulled out and was kneeling in front of me, kissing my just-fucked mouth. This time he savored the press of our lips. "Baby, you're fucking beautiful when you come. And as much as I want to push you onto your back and attack that sweet cunt of yours, we have to go." Regret made his voice tight. "Finnan's waiting."

The reminder that I had to be paraded around at Finnan's pleasure was like having a bucket of cold water over my head. I stood, readjusting my panties and smoothing down the skirts of my dress. In the kitchen, I grabbed my clutch, which stowed a tube of lipstick, clear lip gloss, and a compact.

I took out the lipstick and checked my appearance in the hallway mirror. My lipstick—despite the rough treatment—

had maintained its integrity. I slicked on some lip gloss over the color already there and turned.

Grayson was standing by the closed door, watching me. His eyes drank in all of me, and I could've sworn I felt his gaze like a physical caress. Heat flashed through my body in response—at the memory of his touch. When I approached the door, he drew me to a stop, running his thumb down my bottom lip.

"Your lips wrapped around my cock. It needs to happen again. Nod if you agree with me."

I nodded. God, help me, I nodded because I knew I wouldn't be able to stay away from this man.

"Good." He opened the door and stepped out into the hall. After a moment, he waved me forward. I followed him into the already waiting elevator, feeling the sexual tension between us like a tangible, erotic heat. The muscle in his jaw bulged as if he, too, could feel it. As soon as the doors slid shut, he took me by the wrist and turned me, pressing me against the wall of the elevator car.

"I can't get enough of you," he told me in a strained voice.

The heat of his body felt too hot against my already heated skin. He pinned my arms above my head and rolled his hips against mine. He was hard again.

"Tonight is going to be torture." He growled, nipping my bottom lip—urging me to open for him. He swept his tongue into my mouth. "Not being able to touch you will drive me to the edge of insanity." His voice was rasping and low, lighting up my nerve endings with its timbre. It sounded like sex—if the act of sex could be audible. "But as you sit there for Finnan, I want you to remember the taste of my cum on your tongue. I want you wet and ready for my hard cock to slide between your thighs. And know that every time I look at you from across the table, I'll be thinking about you naked. Thinking about spreading you out, tasting your sweet cunt, and making you scream."

I mewled—the sound high and keening. The pressure of his hips against mine, the control of my arms made my whole body light up with anticipation. With pleasure. With desire.

He slid his hand under the skirt of my dress, gliding it up my thigh until he reached the silk panel of my panties. With his long index finger, he stroked the seam of my pussy.

"I want to be in here so badly. I want to tear these from your hips and sink my rock, hard cock inside you. I want to take you bare because I want to mark you as mine." He pressed a kiss to the side of my mouth and said, "Tell me I can have you bare."

Wordlessly, I nodded, savoring the sweet burn of being captured and held by this man. I rubbed my pussy against his fingers, already picturing everything he described, driving my desire higher and higher.

He pulled his hand out, then brought his fingers to his nose and inhaled.

Heat rushed through me as I watched his eyes shutter closed at my scent.

"Decadent."

His smile was fierce before he released my arms as abruptly as he'd pinned them and stepped away. I was left panting with need, blinking when the elevator doors sprung open. Swallowing down on my lust, I stared at the guards waiting on the ground floor. With his hand on the small of my back, Grayson led me toward the car. Torin had the rear door open already, waiting at ease beside it.

He nodded in deference. "Lass," he said softly as I passed.

"Hi." I slid inside the dark leather interior. Grayson motioned for me to move over, then shut the door behind him. Torin left the parking garage, whisking us out of the artificial light and into the dark night. When we emerged from the underground parking, rain was pattering gently against the windshield and windows.

"Where are we going for dinner?" I asked into the quiet car.

"A place called The Alehouse. It's not too far from where we went to lunch."

I nodded and stared out the window, watching the harbor slide past the glass—blurred into obscurity in the rain. In the reflection, I caught Grayson staring at me with an almost starved look.

Then, I remembered the words he had said to me in the elevator.

Tonight is going to be torture. Not being able to touch you will drive me to the edge of insanity. But as you sit there for Finnan, I want you to remember the taste of my cum on your tongue. I want you wet and ready for my hard cock to slide between your thighs. And know that every time I look at you from across the table, I'll be thinking about you naked. Thinking about spreading you out, tasting your sweet cunt and making you scream.

Oh, God.

I squeezed my thighs together, hoping he didn't notice. Everything about what had happened in the last thirty minutes guaranteed I'd be squirming in my seat through this whole dinner. I only just managed to stifle the soft moan that shot out of my throat as I was jostled in my seat by uneven road. The unexpected friction coupled with my wayward thoughts meant I was wound too tight.

The car eventually drew to a stop at the curb, and the slap of cold air when my door opened a moment later was just what I needed to clear my head. I turned to Torin to find his eyes scanning the surrounding street. He had one hand held out to me and the other tucked into the inside of his jacket. Placing my hand in his, I stepped free of the car, shivering in the night air.

Behind me, the rear door opened and closed, and Grayson eased around the trunk of the black Rover. Flanked by both men, we walked into the restaurant. Torin peeled away as I stepped through, leaving me to be enveloped by the warmth of a wood fire and the scent of garlic and oregano.

A red-headed hostess with a spray of pale brown freckles over her nose and cheeks greeted us at the door. "Your table is ready for you, Mr. Kent," she said. "If you'd like to follow me?"

I followed her with Grayson tight to my ass—using his body as a shield. The other diners looked up as we passed but quickly averted their eyes once they saw who it was.

The table we stopped at was set for nine people.

"Jesus, who else is coming?"

Grayson pulled out a chair for me at the foot of the table, gesturing me to sit. Smoothing my dress under my ass, I hovered over the seat until he could slide it all the way in.

"The upper echelon of the clan."

"And who are you? Are you part of the upper echelon or simply a meat shield?"

A small smile curved the corner of his mouth as he took the seat to my left. "The Warlord for the Mac Tíre Clan."

"The Warlord," I murmured. "What does the Warlord do?"

He settled into his chair, fixing those blue eyes of his on my face. "Traditionally, the Warlord is the head enforcer and primary strategist. He's also responsible for keeping other clan members in line, but my role is slightly different."

"In what way?"

"In the way that I'm more of a personal guard to Finnan."

I felt my eyes widen. "A personal guard? How did that happen?"

"It's a long story."

"We've got time."

Narrowing his eyes on my face, he licked his lips and said, "I saved Finnan's life."

"And you were rewarded with this job as his personal guard?"

"Yes."

"Correct me if I'm wrong, but you haven't been spending a lot of time with him lately. How can you be his personal guard if you've been with me?"

"You're now an extension of Finnan."

"An extension, huh?"

"You're very important to him, Sloane. He's giving up his guard for you."

"Am I supposed to find that romantic?"

"You should. He's risking his life to protect yours."

I didn't know what to say to that, so I said nothing. Clearing my throat, I asked, "Who else is coming to dinner tonight? Any other Warlords?"

A muscle in his jaw flexed. "No."

"Who then?"

Loud voices from the front of the restaurant drew my attention. Five men strolled between the tables, heading in our direction. Each of them radiated malice and danger.

Grayson stood, greeting each man in turn. It started with a firm handshake before they pulled together for a brief hug that involved a lot of thumping on the back.

I remained in my seat until all eyes turned to me. I met each of their stares boldly. Clearly, introductions were not going to be made yet.

A waiter appeared as the men sat down. "Can I get you all some drinks?"

"A bottle of the Macallan Rare Cask. Eight glasses," Grayson said.

"And for the lady?" the man looked at me.

"She'll have a glass of Cristal."

"We only sell it by the bottle, sir," the waiter said, almost apologetically.

Irritation flashing onto his face, Grayson replied, "A bottle then."

From the corner of my eye, I saw Finnan walk in with another man behind him. The rest of the men greeted their leader in the same way they had each other. When it was all over, he walked to me and held out his hand.

With gritted teeth, I forced a smile and took it. Leaning down, he kissed the back of my hand. His kiss may have been chaste, but the lingering look he gave my breasts was not.

"Sloane, you look good enough to eat." His gaze flickered to Grayson as he straightened before he addressed the whole table. "I apologize for my lateness, but I just had a very interesting phone call with Sean Doyle. He upped his offer to a million Euros."

The men began slapping Grayson on the back in congratulations.

"How did you do it?" Finnan asked.

"Leverage," was all he said in reply.

Obviously happy with that answer, he clapped him on the shoulder, then walked around to the head of the table and took a seat. All the other men followed, leaving the single clan member who had come in with Finnan standing.

"Trigger, stay in the car. I think we're safe enough here."

The man—Trigger—bobbed his head and disappeared.

The waiter returned with the drinks Grayson had ordered and set them on the table. He poured me a glass of champagne, then placed the golden bottle into a bucket of ice beside the table before pouring the whisky and distributing the glasses around the table.

When everyone had a drink, Finnan stood and held his glass aloft. "To the Mac Tíre Clan."

The men echoed him, and I took a gulp of my champagne. I thought that was the end of it until Finnan said, "Sloane, would you please stand?"

Placing down my glass, I did as he bid and got to my feet.

"Gentlemen, some of you have heard that I was recently engaged. Let me introduce you to the woman who will ensure the Mac Tíre Clan dominates Ireland for many more years to come. Sloane Kavanaugh, daughter of the American-Irish Mafia Boss, Aidan Kavanaugh."

I felt like a fucking contestant in a beauty pageant. The men dipped their chins in greeting as they were introduced to me.

"Orin Lynch, our clan's Reaper. Caolan Daley, Quartermaster. Shay O'Leary and his twin brother Quillen, Bonebreaker and General. The man next to you is Keir, our Chief and my second-in-command."

"Hello," I said.

"And Grayson, you already know," Finnan added, gesturing to the man on my left. Grayson's piercing blue eyes were on me as he rubbed his index and middle fingers over his mouth. I flushed at the reminder and cleared my throat. I wasn't sure how to play this. I'd been sold and abducted, so it wasn't like I had any choice in the matter when it came to being here.

I could either make my life easier or harder.

I chose easier.

Smiling, I addressed everyone at the table. "It's a pleasure to meet you all."

"Sloane will be accompanying us to the Conclave tomorrow night," Finnan announced with a smug smile.

I opened my mouth to ask what the Conclave was when a waiter appeared with a selection of sharing plates. He placed them down, then whisked away to get the side plates.

All the men fell into easy conversation with each other, and I realized this was less a business dinner and more a family affair.

"Are you okay?" Grayson asked, and I snapped out of my head.

I turned to look at him. "Ah, yes. Fine. Thank you."

He nodded to my plate, where food had miraculously appeared. "You need to eat."

Spearing a forkful of meat, I glanced around at all the men. Orin Lynch looked just as I expected a hitman to look—hard and unyielding. Scary, even. His black hair and eyes made him seem like some dark angel of death. He was speaking with both Shay and Quillen. Caolan and Keir were ribbing each other, which left Finnan staring at me from across the length of the table.

He didn't say anything—simply stared—until there was a panicked shout from the front of the restaurant.

I turned my head, and time seemed to slow. Trigger was running toward us, yelling something I couldn't understand in Gaelic. Grayson understood though, grabbing and dragging me from my chair and under the table a second before an explosion erupted through the restaurant, shattering the front windows. Scorching heat and high-pitched screams filled the air. Glass tinkled as it scattered on the floor.

Heat seared through the restaurant, and my lungs burned as all the air inside was sucked out in the backdraft. Coughing, I tried to drag more oxygen in and rose to my knees.

"Get down, lass," Grayson barked, taking me by the back of the neck and pushing me to the floor.

Why couldn't I focus on his face? I looked up to see every member of the clan crouched under the tables, guns naked in their hands. Finnan was barking orders, Orin moving like he was as insubstantial as smoke as he left the cover of the table. The twins moved as one unit too.

"Grayson, get her to the compound. Now!" Finnan snarled, sliding out from beneath the table with his Glock up and ready.

Grayson took me by the arm and pulled me out. I could see the extent of the damage now. The whole front of the restaurant had been blown apart. Outside was the blackened shell of a van that looked as if it had been split in two from the inside out. Glass and bricks littered the ground, as well as furniture and the bodies of the diners who had been sitting the closest to the window.

As Grayson tugged me away, I craned my neck to see the twisted limbs of the red-head who had seated us. She was dead.

"Sloane!" Grayson yelled. I turned, and he cupped my cheeks, making sure I was focused on his face. "We have to go. *Now.*"

Taking my hand, he entered the kitchen. The chefs and waitstaff looked shell-shocked as we pushed past them on the way to the service entrance. Outside, the air was crisp and cold—a complete contrast to the heat and destruction inside. I shivered, following Grayson to one of the clan's black Rovers parked at the rear.

Pulling open the door, he ushered me inside, then slammed it behind me. Huddled in the middle seat, I wrapped my arms around myself and felt the tremors wracking my body. My father had trained me to survive kidnappings, drugging, having a gun pulled on me, and hand-to-hand combat with an opponent three times larger than me, but he had not prepared me for a car bomb.

"Are you okay, lass?" Grayson asked, looking at me through the rearview mirror. "Sloane?"

"I think I'm going into shock," I mumbled, another great shiver wracking my body.

The skin around his eyes tightened as he cursed under his breath and started the engine. Hitting the gas, he tore out from behind the building and onto the street. I heard wailing sirens coming our way, the bright yellow ambulances zooming past us so quickly the car shook in their wake.

"Talk to me, Sloane. Are you okay?"

I refocused my eyes on Grayson. "What?"

Risking a glance at me, I saw the hard lines branching out from the corners of his mouth and eyes. "Fuck."

I was so cold—colder than I'd ever been in my life. The roar of the engine got louder, and I heard Grayson's voice.

"You're fine, Sloane. You hear me? You didn't get hurt. You're fine."

I stared at him from my position in the rear seat, watching the way he calmly and confidently controlled the car.

"Sloane, talk to me. Tell me you understand."

"I-I u-u-understand." Dammit, my teeth were chattering so much I could hardly talk.

"We'll be there soon. Once I have you to safety, I'll get you into the shower. Warm you up. You'll be fine."

I wiped a shaking hand across my face, shoving the hair from my eyes. The car began to slow, and I peered out the window to find Grayson was pulling into a long driveway. Gravel pinged against the undercarriage and large, dark masses crowded against the glass on either side, but I had no idea whether it was a wall or something softer like a hedge.

"Where are we?" I asked, careful to make sure my teeth weren't chattering too loudly.

"Our clan's safehouse. Oranmore." He glanced at me over his shoulder quickly, then back. "*Shit.*" Braking heavily, he raced from the driver's seat and popped open my door. Grayson took one look at my face and cursed again. "Where are you bleeding?"

"Bleeding?" I asked. I *did* feel lightheaded. Was that because of blood loss, or was that from the shock or surviving a car bomb?

Hauling me into his arms, he kicked shut the door, then marched up to the entrance of the imposing building. I caught a brief glimpse of an ancient-looking flagstone floor almost completely covered by large modern area rugs to keep the chill out of the room.

"What happened?" someone asked.

"Bomb," Grayson replied through gritted teeth. "Is her room ready?"

"Second door on the right," the person replied, then Grayson was powering up the old oak staircase. Like the man, Grayson's gait was rock-steady as he walked down a hallway that was covered in the same dark paneling as the staircase. Portraits hung from the walls, many of which were surrounded by bulky, aged-gilt frames.

Nudging open a door, he stepped into the room and closed us in. Across the vast distance was the bathroom, where he settled me onto the closed lid of the toilet. Dropping into a crouch, he touched my forehead, the pads of his fingers coming back red.

"Fuck, lass." He searched for the wound at my hairline,

his face twisting into fierce concentration as he scraped back my hair. "Where does it hurt?"

"Nowhere," I replied, coughing.

"Then where has the fucking blood come from?" he demanded.

I shook my head and wrapped my arms around me. My right hand slipped off though, and I blinked down at the red smear that had been left behind on my bicep.

Grayson pounced on the injury, gripping my hand and spreading my fingers wide. The stretch across my palm made me suck in a hissed breath, and I tried to pull away, but he kept his grip firm.

"There's glass in there," he announced, then stood to open one of the under-sink cupboards. He pulled out a first-aid kit and ripped open the zipper. Bandages, saline tubes, and alcohol swabs burst out onto the marble floor. He rummaged through until he found a pair of tweezers still in their sterile packaging and ripped them open.

Clutching my hand, he began to pull the glass free from the wound, dropping it onto the marble.

Four pieces of glass—three slivers and one about the size of a dime—sat in a puddle of blood.

Snipping the end off the saline tube, Grayson led me to the sink and flushed the wound before putting on a non-stick dressing and securing it in place.

"How does it feel?" he asked in a rasping voice.

"I can't feel it."

He grunted. "That'll change in the morning." His face had yet to lose that stern concentration as he eyed the bloody smears on my forehead. "Take a seat in the shower."

I turned to see that there was a step built into the stall. "Why?"

He gestured to the mirror behind him, and I got the first look at myself. My face was white—ghostly pale. That was what struck me first. Then it was the blood that stood out in stark contrast, smeared all over my forehead and ear from where I shoved my loose hair.

"I'm going to put you to bed, but I need to clean you off first."

"Why do I need to be in the shower, then?"

"I think you might fall over any moment now, and I need an easy clean-up." He took me by the arm. "Come on. I'll help you."

Shuffling with him, I stepped into the stall and sat. His hand felt incredibly warm against my cold skin, and I whimpered a little when he released his hold.

He frowned. "You're ice-cold." Turning, he pushed the showerhead back to avoid soaking us completely and started the water. Taking a face cloth from the niche in the wall, he wet it thoroughly, then turned around, crouching in front of me.

The water—despite being turned away from us—was creeping along the tile, soaking the knees of his slacks. That was when I noticed my feet were bare. My shoes must've come off when Grayson was getting me out of the restaurant.

"Your clothes are getting wet," I pointed out, my gaze flickering back to his concerned face.

Grayson was wiping away the blood, concentrating so hard that creases formed between his brows. He wet the face cloth again, wringing out the blood. Pink water gurgled down the drain, and he returned to his ministrations.

Once he was satisfied I was clean, he shut off the water and helped me stand. With slow, soft movements, he wiped the water from my face, dried my feet, then scooped me into his arms. His muscles flexed beneath the fabric of his shirt and under the backs of my knees as he walked me to the bed. I noticed for the first time the thick dark blue comforter and matching drapes that could be closed around the four posts. Setting me on my feet, he took off my dress, garter, and thigh-highs—leaving me in nothing but my panties, which had somehow not gotten wet in the shower. His dark gaze roved over my semi-nakedness for a moment, his jaw tight. With a shake of his head, he threw back the blankets.

"Get in, Sloane."

I slid under the sheets, and he took a minute to settle the blankets into place once more. Conflict lay in every line on his face, in every tight muscle.

Eventually, he rasped, "Get some rest, lass," and left.

17

GRAYSON

ORIN HAD WORKED QUICKLY, TRACKING DOWN a guy who had been seen fleeing the scene of the restaurant bombing and bringing him back to the warehouse for questioning. Now, he sat on a steel chair in the middle of a vast, open space while the clan members stood around him.

Blood had begun to pool beneath the chair, dripping from wounds I couldn't distinguish given how well he'd been worked over.

"Who is he?" Finnan asked, his arms folded over his chest while he watched our captive barely breathe.

"He passed out before I could ask him," Orin replied, his tone serial-killer bleak.

"And it's not like we can ask him now," Shay added, staring at the mass of blood and bruises. "You cut out his tongue."

Orin shrugged like it was no big deal. Removing the tongue of our enemies was his MO. "He still has functioning fingers."

"At least he did until Quillen got to him," Caolan added helpfully.

I glanced down at the man's bloody hands and noticed that at least two fingers were angled badly, and one was missing. "He's still got his left hand," I pointed out.

"I hate sloppy penmanship," Keir commented absently, cocking his head to one side.

"What did you get out of him before he passed out?" Finnan demanded, uncrossing his arms and stepping closer.

"He didn't say much before 'fuck you' and 'you'll have to kill me first,'" Orin replied. "As you can see, I didn't appreciate those answers very much."

Shay and Quillen chuckled darkly.

"He never said who had ordered the hit," Orin tacked on, frowning at the unconscious man. He turned to Finnan. "Want me to dispose of him?"

The boss nodded. "Make it messy. I want his body found, and whoever sent him to know that we're coming for them as soon as we learn who they are."

The Reaper leaned down to put his shoulder against the would-be car bomber—or assistant car bomber—and hauled him out of the seat and over his powerful shoulder. Knowing Orin, it wouldn't be a bullet to the brain. He would choose a more drawn-out process—especially if his quarry was still alive.

Finnan clapped me on the back but spoke to everyone remaining. "Now, who wants to go and get their dicks sucked to celebrate surviving this fucking attempt."

THIRTY MINUTES LATER, WE FILED INTO VELVET, AND I could feel each man's need for sexual release press against my skin. As soon as we stepped through the door, the regular girls flocked to their favorite clan member, half of them being guided to the private rooms while the other half—including Finnan—went to the bar to enjoy a drink first.

I hung back for a moment to speak to Little John.

"How'd you go with that issue the other day?"

"The pigs are eating well," was all he said in reply, and that was enough.

Nobody was finding the body of Kitty's ex anytime soon.

"Hey, daddy," Rhapsody said. "Come out back and I'll take care of you." She tugged at my hand, but I yanked it out of her grasp. Undeterred, she crooked her finger at me. "Come on, Grayson. I can take care of that hard cock of yours."

I had no interest in being with this woman who had warmed my bed in the past. What I wanted was a certain sass-mouthed Yank. I turned when I felt eyes on me, finding Finnan's green eyes locked on my face. *Fuck.*

"Watch our backs," I said to Little John as I was left with no choice but to follow Rhapsody.

The other man nodded, then got busy scanning the club.

When we got to a spare room, she shut us in and pushed me onto the semi-circular leather seat. In the middle of the room was a black polished podium, a silver pole centered and bolted into the ceiling.

"Want me to dance for you, daddy?" Rhapsody asked. I didn't reply, and she took my silence as agreement, stepping onto the raised platform on her seventeen-centimeter-high black leather pleasers that went all the way up past her knees. I watched her move with the music, gyrating around for my entertainment, and I felt...

Nothing.

Not a damn thing.

She pressed her tits together, licking the valley between. "You like that, daddy?" she asked in a throaty purr.

I continued to watch her roll her hips, spread her legs, and wiggle her ass at me, but that empty feeling never went away. If anything, the hollowness began to feel as big as a fucking chasm. It was clear to Rhapsody that I wasn't reacting the way she wanted me to because she pouted and looked at my crotch. I glanced down too, wondering whether I'd missed something.

She dropped down in a squat, her legs spread wide, her pussy visible through the gaping holes in the sides of her panties. "Want me to suck that dick?" She grinned and placed her hands down, crawling to me. "You want my mouth all over it? Come on, daddy," she cajoled, sliding from the podium and down onto her knees between my legs.

With practiced movement, she undid my belt buckle, flicked open the button, and pulled down the zipper. My cock did not spring out to greet her. It lay flaccid and unimpressed in my boxer briefs.

"Got a bit of performance anxiety?" She pouted again—her signature move. "I can help you with that."

She began to stroke me, then proceeded to stuff my limp dick in her mouth as she attempted to coax it to life. The thing was, it had had Sloane's lips around it before, and nothing could compare to that. It knew that Rhapsody was a weak imitation of what it had once had and refused to rise to the occasion.

The fact that I was thinking about my dick in the third person was the straw that broke the camel's back. With my hands on her shoulders, I pushed her back gently.

A frown wrinkled her brow. "What's wrong, daddy?"

"I'm just not in the mood."

She pursed her lips, the frown deepening. "But you love my blow jobs."

"I don't love them, Rhapsody. A man's dick is going to get hard if a beautiful woman's mouth is near it."

She eyed my limp dick, which I tucked back into my slacks and zipped up. "So, why isn't your dick getting hard?"

I shrugged and stood, forcing her to shuffle backward on her knees.

Then I did something I'd never done before.

Reaching into my pocket, I handed her a wad of cash. "Sorry, baby. I'm just not in the mood tonight."

She stared at her fistful of Euros, then back at me, her expression clouding with something I had never seen on her face before—rage. "Is it that other woman?"

Inside, I froze.

Outside, I turned to her with a bored expression. "What other woman?"

"The one I saw you coming out of the bathroom with at *Foundry*."

For a moment, all the muscles in my body locked down tight. "I don't know what you're talking about."

"Yeah, you do." She rose to her feet effortlessly, a smug tilt on her lips. "She was a knockout with platinum hair and a black dress. I was *there*. I saw her. I saw you two together."

I couldn't let Rhapsody see that her having this knowledge was making me sweat. Clearly, she had no idea who Sloane really was, but all she had to do was ask around, and she would find out.

I knew I shouldn't react, but the idea of someone threatening Sloane was making me so insane that I couldn't see straight. "You didn't see shit, Rhapsody." My words came out as a hiss, and I stepped toward her. My hand had wrapped around the grip of my gun, and I pulled it out.

She put her hands up, all self-satisfaction gone from her face. Her wide eyes darted between my face and the muzzle of the gun. "Grayson, what are you doing?"

I gave her my best blank expression. "You didn't see shit, Rhapsody." I put my finger on the trigger. "Repeat those words back."

"I didn't see shit," she said, her words soft—threaded with fear.

"That's right. You're going to keep your fucking mouth shut about what you *thought* you saw. You understand?"

"I understand." Running her tongue across her top lip, she said, "How much would you pay me to keep my silence?"

What. The. Fuck.

I narrowed my eyes. "You didn't just attempt to blackmail

me, did you, Rhapsody? Because if you did, that was a big fucking mistake."

Backpedaling, she started to say, "I'm sorry, Grayson. I'm sorry." She hid her face in her hands, hunching over her shoulders. And was she *crying*? "I don't know what I was thinking. It's just that my landlord has threatened to kick me out at the end of the month, and I have nowhere to go. If I could just earn a little more money—"

Her words dropped off when I barked a rough, "Fuck." Holstering my weapon, I ran a hand through my hair. "If money is what you need, the fucking clan will provide. You don't need to resort to blackmail."

She peered up at me from her cupped hands, her mascara streaking down her cheeks. "Really?"

I shook my head. "Aye. Really." Heaving a sigh, I looked up at the ceiling for a moment before telling her, "Get fucking cleaned up."

Opening the door, I strolled down the hallway and back out into the club. I didn't know whether I could trust Rhapsody to keep her fucking mouth shut, but I had to trust that she knew she would end up dead behind a dumpster if she didn't.

When I emerged, the rest of the clan were nowhere to be seen, and I slipped out the door unnoticed.

18

SLOANE

SOME TIME LATER I WOKE UP FEELING TOO HOT. Throwing the thick quilt from my body, I expected the cool kiss of the night air on my skin, but I was still burning up. Opening my eyes fully, I blinked into the darkness, waiting for my eyes to adjust to the slight sliver of light that was coming in from behind the drapes.

An arm tightened around my waist, dragging me into the line of a hard, hot body. For a moment, panic flared until I smelled sandalwood and leather and knew who was wrapped around me. Wordlessly, Grayson tore the panties from my waist, then bent my legs up—like I was sitting in a chair. I felt the blunt head of his erection prodding at my entrance.

"I've tried to stay away, lass," he rasped into my ear, his five o'clock shadow rubbing against my cheek. "But I can't stay away any longer."

He ran his hand around the front of my hip, his fingers finding the place between my legs that he wanted to dominate. He drew my ass in more tightly to his body, letting me feel his erection more firmly.

"I want to fuck into this pussy... just slide right inside your slick cunt, claim you, and make you scream my name while you come all over me."

A breath shuddered out of me as I arched against him. The hand around my waist came to cup my bare breast, his thumb sweeping over my nipple. The action must've been a direct line to my clit, because it began to beat in tandem with the movement of his thumb.

"I know I should leave you the fuck alone. I said I wouldn't take more than a taste of you, but after what happened tonight..." he let out a hissed breath as if finishing the thought caused him pain, "... I'm going to take you bare because I'm a possessive bastard and I need to know that I marked you first. Will your greedy little pussy drink all my cum down, Sloane? Does the idea of me spilling inside you turn you the fuck on?"

"Yes," I whispered, gasping when he shoved inside me without warning.

My breath caught, and I moaned his name. His hand covered my mouth, muffling my words. His chest was hot and hard against my back when he growled into my ear, "Shhh."

After a beat, he moved his hand away from my mouth and down to my neck. His large fingers wrapped around the column of my throat, applying the slightest pressure. With one hand on my hip and the other around my throat,

Grayson fucked into me. Dropping his head to my shoulder, his hot breaths shivered over my skin, turning my already heated body into an inferno.

With my legs folded up close to my body, the sensation of Grayson's cock going in and out of me was amplified. My channel felt tight, and if his groans were anything to go by, it felt tight for him, too. With his fingers wrapped around my throat, slightly constricting the flow of oxygen, I was floating on a cloud of bliss.

"Fuck, you feel good, lass," he whispered into my ear. "I want to own your cunt, to reach the end of you and mark you."

Thrust.

"But I need to get deeper inside you."

I yelped when he pulled out, dragged me on top of him, and forced me to straddle his hips. Lifting me effortlessly, he impaled me on his dick, hitting me deeper than he had before.

I moaned.

"Knowing Finnan will have you in his bed soon drives me insane even now."

Thrust.

"It's a small measure of comfort to know that I was inside your pussy before him."

Thrust.

"I'm going to make sure you remember whose name you screamed when I spill inside you."

Thrust.

Gripping his shoulders, I stared down at his bare chest, realizing my night vision was improving. I could see all the tattoos inked onto his skin. There must've been dozens upon dozens of tattoos made up of the same intricate Celtic knots as the one on his right hand.

Taking advantage, my fingertips skimmed over his fevered skin, hearing the catch in his breath when I did. I explored his chest, feeling the strong, steady thump of his heart under my palm. When I stroked over his left pec, I frowned. His skin wasn't warm and smooth like the rest of his chest. Instead, it was raised and slick.

Grayson wrapped his hand around mine, stopping my exploration.

"What happened?"

He stopped thrusting but kept a grip on my waist so I couldn't move away. "I was shot."

My mouth went dry. "A while ago, right?"

Grayson was quiet for a long moment. "Yes."

"When?"

"Almost ten years now." He released my hand.

Staring into his ice-blue eyes, which looked gray in the low light, I asked, "What happened?"

"I took a bullet for someone."

"Jesus, Grayson. I—"

He shook his head. "I don't want to talk about me now, Sloane. Right now? I want to fuck you. Hard. Without mercy. I want to own your pussy." He punctuated each of his statements by thrusting into me, making my eyes roll into the back of my skull.

"*Christ,*" he swore, flipping me onto my back and bracing himself above me. With a strong hand wrapped around one of my legs, he propped it up onto his shoulder, going deeper still. I felt every ridge of his cock gliding against my sensitive flesh.

I held onto his biceps as he fucked into me, digging my nails into his skin.

"Fuck, you're tight. And wet," he said on a grunt, his cock stroking me relentlessly.

My mouth parted, his name falling from my lips on a whimper. Threading my fingers into his hair, I tugged and whispered, "Faster."

Quickening his thrusts and hitting me deep, he said low and fast, "I will *never* stop wanting you, Sloane. You hear me?" He spoke that last part into my ear, biting down on the lobe and making me shiver. "Even when you're with Finnan. I will always remember this."

I blinked because that had sounded like a goodbye.

Before I could analyze it too closely, he urged, "Now, come, baby. I want to feel your body squeeze mine."

As if on command, all other thoughts fled me, leaving me with one single task—to come on his cock, my body throbbing and thrumming with pleasure.

Grayson's hips increased in pace, his body sliding into mine three more times before he pressed his hips in close to my ass. I felt his cock kick, could feel the pulsing of his balls as they drew up tight to unload inside me.

Lost.

We were both lost in our pleasure together.

And I never wanted to be found again.

19

GRAYSON

SLOANE'S INNER WALLS WERE STILL CLAMPING down on my cock, trying to hold me inside her body for a few seconds more, when I withdrew from her slick heat. I couldn't stay here—in her bed, in her room—even though every instinct I had was telling me to do just that.

I'd crossed the line I swore I never would.

This couldn't happen again.

I sat up, throwing my legs off the side of the bed.

Behind me, Sloane asked, "Where are you going?"

"It's early. Go back to sleep," I told her, turning to look at her over my shoulder. But what I saw nearly broke my resolve to stay away from her. Wrapped loosely in the sheet, her eyes were vulnerable, her body language expressing the things she wouldn't voice.

What had just happened had meant something to her.

And it had fucking meant something to me, too.

I hadn't been prepared for that. For me, a woman was a distraction. Once I got off, and she got off, that was it. Done. Dusted. I would get ghost, and although some would try and reconnect, that wasn't what I was about. How could I consider being responsible for someone else's happiness and well-being when my life was so... violent? Fallon was, of course, the exception to that, and she always would be.

My head told me to get the hell out of there, but when I spied her glistening cunt peeking out through the sheet, I grabbed her ankle and drew her closer. Burying my fingers into her wet pussy, I found my cum warm and wet in her tight sheath, and the knowledge that I'd marked her before *him* was a fucking high like no other. This woman—whether she knew it or not—was mine.

I pumped two fingers in and out, watching the way she lost control. The sheet fell from her body, and I drank my fill. Sloane was pure perfection with her platinum blonde hair, her just-right handful of breasts, slender waist, flared hips, and long, tanned legs.

Planting one hand down onto the bed, I bent and sucked one of her nipples into my mouth, teasing the aching bud with the tip of my tongue. Her skin smelled like me now, and it soothed the possessive side of me. She writhed, her legs scissoring on either side of my hips. Christ, I was hard again, but I couldn't give in. I needed to go.

Easing my fingers out of her pussy, I brought them to her lips. "Taste yourself, and me."

She opened her mouth, sucking in the digits and swirling her tongue around them.

I licked my bottom lip, almost tasting what she was tasting.

"Fucking perfect," I told her, my voice dropping an octave. With a sharp pain lancing my chest, I got dressed, then slipped from her room.

I knew we had to stop this.

I couldn't be involved with the woman who would become Finnan's wife.

I couldn't let myself be drawn in.

My loyalty was supposed to be to Finnan and the Clan, but right this minute, I didn't give a fuck. I didn't give a shit about loyalty or the men I commanded.

For once in my life, I wanted to be selfish.

I wanted her.

I took a quick shower, got into clean clothes, then went to the kitchen, where Torin was nursing a cup of coffee.

I nodded to him as I beelined to the coffee maker.

"Where did you disappear off to?" he asked. "I didn't see you after I was finished with Megs."

"I wasn't in the mood to socialize," I replied. Yeah, I wasn't in the mood for getting my dick sucked by a woman who wasn't Sloane. "I cut away early and came back here."

As if thinking her name had conjured her, Sloane breezed into the kitchen. Even though she was in the same singed and dusty dress I'd taken her out of last night, she looked gorgeous. Her hair was still damp from the shower she'd taken, and some part of me was disappointed that she'd washed away the scent of me—and my cum—from her body.

Jesus, fuck, I was acting like an animal marking my territory. When it came to Sloane, though, I couldn't seem to help it. She *was* mine.

"Coffee, lass?" Torin asked.

"Please."

Torin got busy pouring Sloane a cup of coffee, which she took with a smile. Bringing the mug to her mouth, she stared at me over the rim.

"Where the fuck is she?" Finnan suddenly roared, his voice echoing off the hallway walls. "I need to speak to that *bitch.*" He stormed into the kitchen, his green eyes dark with anger and agitation, fixing on Sloane.

"Finnan?" I asked, placing down my coffee mug and reaching for my gun.

Jabbing a finger in her direction, he snarled, "You. In my office. Now."

Calmly, Sloane placed her coffee mug down, threw her shoulders back, and started after him.

Torin and I shared a look.

"What do you think that's about?" I asked, my heart racing.

Torin drained the rest of his cup and poured another. "Last night at Velvet, when we were sitting down for a drink, he mentioned something about who he suspects is leaking our information."

"And who does he think it is?"

Torin jerked his chin in the direction Finnan and Sloane had gone.

"Sloane?" Yeah, I couldn't keep the fucking shock out of my voice. "He thinks *Sloane* is the rat?"

He shrugged and took a draw off his mug. "He's looking at everyone."

"She's barely been in the country for a week. How could

she be responsible for anything?" *Other than driving me fucking insane*, I tacked on silently.

Torin shrugged. "I dunno. Maybe Finnan thinks her da sent her?"

"This is fucking insane," I snapped. "Who he should be looking at finding is whoever ordered those car bombs."

"I agree." He scrubbed a hand through his hair, suddenly looking wrung out.

"Is everything all right, my brother?"

Torin's dark eyes ratcheted to my face, his eyes settling on mine for a second before lowering. "Fine. Why wouldn't it be?"

I stretched out my neck, trying to loosen some of the tension that had started forming there. I had a suspicion there was a direct correlation between that hitch in my shoulders and Sloane being alone with Finnan—being *interrogated*.

I tried to finish my coffee, but in the end, I dumped what was remaining in my mug into the sink and walked down the hall to Finnan's office.

Stopping outside the door, I leaned against the opposite wall, crossing my arms while I waited. I heard Finnan shouting—the violence of his words punctuated by silence as Sloane either didn't reply or was keeping her cool.

Fuck, what were they talking about? What was being said?

The door to the office suddenly opened and Sloane walked out with her face set into a scowl. She was pissed as fuck, but one look at Finnan behind her, and I knew that it was a group session of being pissed off.

I wanted to ask what had happened when Finnan snarled,

"Get your arse in here."

Sloane flicked me an irritated look, then marched down the hallway.

I stepped into the office and Finnan shut the door behind him with an ominous *click*.

"Sit down."

I took the seat opposite the desk and waited. Finnan paced across the rug behind me, and I slid down in my seat. Waiting.

"It's not her," he finally bit out.

I turned to face him. "Her *who*?" I asked.

"Sloane!" he roared. "She's not the motherfucking rat."

My brows rose. "I didn't know you thought she was. We've been chasing after this rat for months."

He glared at me as he made another revolution of the rug. "I thought her da had sent her." He rounded the desk and sat down. "I need to find out who it is, Grayson, and I need you to find out *right... fucking... now*."

"Yes, boss. Anything else?"

"Yeah. The Conclave is still going ahead tonight."

My shoulders stiffened. "Are you sure that's wise? We were attacked last night. Someone set off two car bombs in the hopes of taking us all out, and you want to go to the Conclave and risk your life again?"

"I won't fucking hide from these motherfuckers!"

"Finnan—"

"And I want Sloane to come with me."

I leaped from my seat, irrational fear sweeping through me. "Are you fucking serious?"

The look he gave me was irritated, bordering on

murderous. "She's my fiancée. Soon, she'll be my wife. I want the rest of the clan bosses to see her. I want them to see that I have Aidan Kavanaugh's daughter."

I loved Finnan, but his ego would be his fucking downfall.

"Finnan, it's too dangerous."

"Leaving her behind is too dangerous," he replied in a snarl. "Those bombs were meant to take both us and Sloane out. She's got just as big of a target on her back as we do now."

My hands curled into fists. There wasn't anything I wouldn't do to keep her safe, but taking her to the Conclave? Finnan had lost his ever-loving mind.

"Boss," I tried one last time.

"My decision is final, Kent. And since you're so fucking concerned for her safety, you'll continue to guard her with your life. Am I understood?"

I ground my molars together. "Understood." I turned to leave, but Finnan stopped me.

"Take her out to buy a new dress for tonight. I want her to look like a million Euros."

I nodded. "Sir." Leaving the office, I turned back toward the kitchen but stopped when I saw Sloane sticking her head out of her room.

"Did he accuse you of being the rat, too?" she asked.

"No, but he said he thought you were."

"He's paranoid. My father is also paranoid."

"Aye. I think it comes with the territory of ruling a clan." I ran a hand through my hair, then down the back of my neck. "We have the Conclave tonight. He wants you to come."

She frowned. "What's a Conclave?"

"It's the meeting between all the clans in Ireland. It's the one night a year when we all come together to share a meal, discuss business, and no violence can occur. If anyone breaks this cardinal rule, that clan is embargoed."

"Meaning?"

"The other clans can seize any of the offending clan's shipments as their own, without fear of retribution." I shrugged. "It's a long-standing tradition among the clan bosses, and it has served us well for the last decade."

"And he wants me to come."

"He wants to brag to the other bosses and chiefs. He—"

She stopped me with a cutting motion. "He wants to show me off. I get it. I'm the prize he can't stop bragging about."

I grunted, acknowledging her statement begrudgingly.

She studied my face, then looked down at the dress she had on last night. "And what am I supposed to wear tonight? I don't have any clothes here."

"I'll take care of it."

I TOOK SLOANE INTO ORANMORE—THE SMALL town a few miles north of the compound. It wouldn't have all the designer labels she was used to wearing, but it was as good as it was going to get—at least for now.

Torin trailed us as I showed her the half dozen clothing stores on the high street. When we finally reached one that Sloane had a vague interest in, I told Torin to go and get something to eat, then come back. We didn't need the extra eyes drawing attention to our location.

A bell signaled our entry into the boutique and caused the assistant to look up from the stock she was sorting through. "Hello, Mr. Kent. Can I help you with anything today?"

"My friend here needs a dress for tonight, as well as some casual clothes. Can you help her?"

The woman smiled. "Of course." She approached Sloane with that friendly smile still in place. "My name's Maeve."

"Sloane."

"What size are you, Sloane?"

She bit her bottom lip, making me groan. "I'm not sure. The sizes are different from in the States."

"She's an eight," I provided.

Maeve nodded and took Sloane by the arm, leading her toward some racks with long evening-style dresses. Taking a seat in the plush chair that was positioned facing the changing room, I watched the two women discuss their options, setting aside some dresses and discarding others.

"That one," I said, pointing at the ugly-as-fuck, full-length, shapeless, long-sleeved, dress.

Sloane looked over at it, her mouth puckering. "You can't be serious."

But Maeve dutifully added it to the collection to try on while Sloane glared at me.

When there were half a dozen dresses on the hook in the dressing room, Sloane stepped inside to start trying them on. When the dress she was wearing hit the floor, I shifted uneasily in my seat. Knowing she was in nothing but the bra she had on yesterday was torture to my already hard dick.

A few minutes passed before she drew back the curtain, showing off the first option.

I inched forward in my chair.

The silvery fabric clung to every one of Sloane's curves, highlighting her breasts, hips, and long legs. The hem sat at least seven inches above her knee, while a fringed hem covered the next couple of inches of her thighs.

She looked fucking phenomenal, but I didn't want everyone to see her like that.

"Not that one," I told her, my voice thick. "Try on the one I chose."

She fucking pouted, and I wanted to take her over my knee. "I like this one."

Fuck, so do I. But I was in serious danger of shooting every motherfucker who laid eyes on her if she wore it.

"My choice."

She glowered at me as she stepped back inside the changing room and drew the curtain.

As she changed into the next dress, I ground my molars together, thinking about Finnan's ridiculous desire to show Sloane off when there was clearly more than one threat hovering over our heads.

When the curtain rippled again and Sloane drew the fabric back, I eyed the dress I'd picked out for her. It was a horrible shade of dark yellow, so it clashed with her pale skin and nearly silver hair. The yards of fabric helped hide her body, and with that, it also saved me from shooting people in the face.

"That one," I said.

She arched a brow. "Did you get hit on the head while I was in there?" She plucked at the fabric over her stomach. "This is hideous."

"Maybe, but it'll mean people won't stare at you."

She blinked at me, cocking her head to the side. "You want me to look ugly so people don't stare?"

My jaw bulged with a barely restrained desire to push her up against the mirror and fuck her into submission. Instead, I shifted in my seat again. "Yes."

Sloane shook her head. "That's messed up... even for you, Grayson." Enclosing herself once more, she tried on the other dresses but refused to come out and show me.

Maeve started dropping off jeans and t-shirts, skirts and jackets—carefully building her a more complete wardrobe. When Sloane finally emerged dressed in jeans and a loose-fitting t-shirt and with an armful of clothes, she took them to the counter. Glancing over my shoulder, I saw that she'd left the yellow dress behind.

Fuck, this woman was going to be the death of me.

"You left something behind," I told her.

She flicked her gaze in the direction of the changing room then back to me. "No, I didn't. I'm not wearing that dress. I'd rather go naked."

I chewed the inside of my cheek, desperately trying to keep my cool.

Maeve gave me the tally for everything, and I paid her in cash. As soon as I got outside, I gave the bags to Torin, leaving my hands free in case I needed to reach for my gun.

"I need new panties and bras," Sloane said.

Torin's head turned at the sound of those two keywords, and I slapped him over the back of the head. "Gobshite," I muttered. Then to Sloane, I said, "There's a lingerie store across the road."

Turning to Torin, I told him, "Take the bags to the car."

His dark eyes flickered to the front door of the lingerie store. "I just got a wicked feeling of déjà vu."

I grunted. "Me too. I'll make sure—"

His phone rang, and he looked at the number, the color draining from his face.

"Do you have to take that?"

"Yeah," he replied, still staring at the screen. When he looked back, he added, "I'll take these bags back and come back for you in thirty."

Before I could respond, Torin started hurrying up the road.

Scanning the street, I escorted Sloane to the shop, stepped inside, and locked the door. The young woman manning the counter glanced from Sloane to me—her eyes widening when she realized who I was.

"G-good m-m-morning, Mr. Kent," she stammered, wringing her hands together in front of her. "Can I help you find anything today?"

"Not me." I jerked my chin in Sloane's direction. "Her. Get her whatever she needs. No limits."

The girl dropped into a curtsey. "Of course."

There was another one of those plush chairs for waiting husbands, and I took a seat. My cock stirred and thickened behind my zipper as I remembered the last time Sloane and

I had been in a lingerie store together.

The women moved around the perimeter of the store, picking out different panties and bras and then hanging the selections up to try.

As soon as Sloane stepped into the changing room, I dismissed the girl, telling her to lock the store behind her.

"What was that?" Sloane called.

"Nothing," I said. Impatient to have my hands on her again, I shoved aside the curtain and stepped inside, letting the fabric fall back into place behind me.

Sloane was completely naked, except for her panties, and a groan rumbled deep from my chest.

"Christ, lass."

Her mouth parted.

Pinning her arms above her head, I held them against the mirror, making her arch her back and stick out her fantastic tits. I let her see the feral, possessive side of me peer out.

She released a shuddered breath.

Leaning down, I sucked one of her nipples into my mouth, causing the already rigid peak to harden even further. Switching my attention to her other breast, I gave her other nipple the same treatment, pressing her wrists more tightly to the mirror. I wanted her caged in with no escape. Transferring both of her hands into one of mine, I reached down between her legs and found her soaked.

Into her ear, I growled, "I'm going to take you, Sloane. Hard. Fast. Dirty. Right here."

She mewled, jutting her breasts out even more.

Lowering the zipper of my slacks, I pulled my cock free

and dragged it through her slick pussy. Her whole body trembled, and she widened her stance.

Fuck, I needed both my hands on her. Glancing up, I saw a railing—one that was designed to have hangers hooked onto it—bolted to the wall. Guiding her hands into place, I told her, "Hang on. Don't take your hands off, or I'll take my belt to your sweet ass."

She blinked at me with longing in her eyes, and I smiled. She liked that idea.

"You want me to spank you, my dirty girl?"

She writhed. Moaned. Begged me wordlessly to do it.

Gripping the end of my belt, I pulled it through the loops of my slacks slowly, heightening her senses with the soft *swoosh* of the leather. "Turn around."

Sloane repositioned herself to face the mirror, her arms still stretched above her head. Folding the belt over itself, I created a loop of leather, running it gently over her sensitive flesh. Her hips flexed like it was my cock between her thighs.

Drawing back a few inches, I flicked the end of the belt at her right ass cheek, my dick twitching with the crack of leather and the sweet moan that followed. I repeated the stroke on her left ass cheek, soothing the sting away with my palm. Her skin already felt hot from the strikes, and the tip of my dick wept.

"Again," she moaned, sticking her ass out as an offering. "Again. Please."

I struck her twice more on each cheek, rubbing and massaging the pain away an instant later. Her ass had taken on a lovely shade of pink.

My dick was like a steel bat now. I pressed into her, crowding her against the mirror. My dick—impatient to get inside her—slid in between her legs. Reaching down, I positioned the blunt head at her opening and pushed inside. Her cunt was slick with desire, with need, with fucking wanting.

Fucking into her, I reached around and rubbed her clit, staring at our reflection in the mirror. Her face was slack, her eyes shut, as she gave herself up to my body. My other hand wrapped around her throat, my thumb pressing into the pounding pulse at the side of her neck.

I thrust into her, my pace slow and deep and possessive. I wanted her sore after this, to think about it at dinner. With my mouth on the other side of her neck, I kissed her slowly. She tasted like vanilla again, and I fucking savored it.

Her inner muscles started to contract, and I knew she was close. Releasing my hold on her throat, I leaned forward and bit the side of her neck. A shudder wracked through her. I couldn't believe this beautiful creature was letting me possess her like this. *Possession.* That was what I wanted. Complete and utter possession of her. I didn't want to share her.

I didn't want to give her up.

"Grayson, please," she whimpered. "Make me come."

With renewed effort, I sank into her as far as I could before pulling back and slamming into her once more. My balls slapped at the front of her pussy from the force of my thrusts, and the sound of our sex—my grunts, her moans—shoved me over the edge.

We came together, my orgasm setting off hers—her inner walls milking my cock, greedily, accepting every last drop of my cum. Her arms were shaking when I finally came down from the euphoric high. Reaching up, I unhooked her fingers and turned her in my arms. Her expression was slack, her mouth open, her eyes heavy-lidded.

"You're mine, Sloane," I whispered fiercely against her mouth. "I don't give a fuck about Finnan. Or my duty to the clan. You. Are. Mine."

20

SLOANE

AS I SLIPPED INTO THE SILVER DRESS FOR THE Conclave, my mind replayed what had happened in the fitting room. Grayson and I certainly had a thing for public fucking. Public fucking in lingerie stores. My pussy was still sore from the pounding it had received, but I relished the ache between my thighs. It reminded me that Grayson was so desperate to be inside me that he temporarily lost himself.

You're mine, Sloane.

Christ, even his possessive words made me wet.

I'd just shut the closet when there was a knock on my bedroom door. Grayson stood on the other side, wearing another suit. I let my gaze drop to take him all in and knew that beneath all that fabric was a man who knew how to fuck.

"Keep looking at me like that, lass, and I'll have to take

you against the wall."

My gaze flickered back to his, finding it hungry. Walking back inside, I made sure to swing my hips more than necessary—making the tasseled hem flare—and sat on the edge of my bed while he watched from the doorway.

Knowing I was flashing the tops of my thigh-highs, I slid on the new shoes that we'd picked up today in town, then asked, "Where's the Conclave happening?"

His blue eyes darted from my legs to my face. "In the only neutral location we have. A town called Athlone. It's about an hour away. Come on, or we'll be late."

"Is Finnan coming with us?"

"No, he wants to arrive last. Call it a..." his mouth dipped into an irritated scowl, "... powerplay on his end."

WHEN WE PULLED UP TO THE RESTAURANT AN HOUR later, I peered out the rain-lined passenger window to find a restaurant not too dissimilar to the one Grayson had taken me to for lunch in Galway.

I waited for Torin to open my door, then stepped out onto the sidewalk. The bottom of my dress rode up and slid along the seat, flashing the lace tops of my thigh-highs. Torin cleared his throat abruptly and averted his gaze.

"Sorry," I said to him softly.

His eyes darted to my face before turning away again. "Please don't mention this to Grayson. He'll have my head."

I smiled. "Your secret is safe with me."

He winked at me, then straightened when Grayson

rounded the back of the Rover.

"Why the fuck are you winking at her?" he barked at Torin.

Torin's shoulders squared, and he said, "No reason."

For a tense moment, he stared at the other man, choosing to let it go when I shivered a little.

Grayson swung his serious eyes to me. "You're cold?"

I gestured to the dress. "It's kind of hard *not* to be cold in this dress."

He grunted, saying in a voice so low it was only meant for my ears, "That fucking dress."

Placing his hand on the small of my back, he led me into the restaurant while Torin took up the rear.

The hostess was waiting for us when we stepped inside. It was clear she didn't know where to look because her brown eyes couldn't settle on anyone's face. She finally pulled herself together enough to say, "You're the first to arrive, sir. I'll show you to your table."

"Stay with the car," Grayson growled to Torin before he escorted me to our table.

The restaurant itself felt impersonal compared to the other one Grayson had taken me to. The décor was sleek and modern. Glass, brushed metal, and a lot of steel made up the tables and chairs. The walls were white, and instead of warm lighting, it was cold and somehow hostile.

The hostess stopped at a large table at the back of the restaurant. It was as far from the kitchen and restrooms as you could get, which would guarantee privacy. Grayson pulled out a chair that put my back to the restaurant, and while I got settled, I watched the hostess's eyes gravitate toward him.

"I'll send the waiter over to take your drink order," she said, finally disappearing back to the hostess stand.

Grayson was only in his seat for a moment when his whole demeanor changed. Aggression seemed to breathe from his body as he stared at something across the other side of the room. A quick glance over my shoulder, and I learned why.

A man that carried the same sort of menacing energy as Grayson had entered the restaurant. He was beginning to go bald, his red hair sparse over the top of his head. Eyes the color of sapphires stared out at me, and like the stone I associated them with, they were hard and austere. Behind him trailed another man who was as unremarkable as he could get. Brown eyes. Brown hair. No distinguishing features, although he did have an intense stare.

I looked over at Grayson, hoping to get some information, but he simply shook his head, his jaw vice-tight.

Another man arrived then. He had a receding hairline and a jagged scar running from above his eye socket to the corner of his mouth. He was followed in by a much younger man who had the same fair hair as him.

Next came a man whose dark hair was speckled with gray. Out of all the men, he looked to be the oldest, although there was a tinge of grayness to his skin that nudged at ill health. His eyes were so dark they were almost black, but it was the young beautiful, blonde woman who walked beside him that held my attention. With intelligent green eyes, she was wearing a gown that sparkled and shimmered with thousands of crystals sewn into the bodice.

Just as the blonde was being shown to her chair, another

two men entered the restaurant. One had hair so dark it looked blue in the bright lights, his eyes the same startling blue as Grayson's.

The man walking beside him had a mop of strawberry blond curls that were long enough to be pulled back into a ponytail. Freckles spattered the bridge of his nose while cool blue eyes stared at me before flickering to the blonde.

I chanced a glance at Grayson, seeing the tension in his shoulders as he stared at the collection of men and women in front of him. *Where in the hell was Finnan?*

Just then, the man in question swaggered into the restaurant, wearing a smile that resembled the cat who ate the canary. Behind him was Keir.

Mine and Finnan's eyes met from across the room, and his smile turned devious.

He approached the table. "Sloane, my diamond, you look radiant."

That name. I hated it. It was what I'd been called during the auction. I guessed now I knew why it had been used. It was clearly a code word.

Finnan held out his hand to me, but in order to place my hand in his, I had to rise from my chair. As I stood, I got a distinct impression that he wanted to show me off—to parade me about so the other men could see me.

Sure enough, as soon as I was close, he took me by the elbow and steered me to face the other men.

"Gentleman, allow me to introduce you to Miss Sloane Kavanaugh." Finnan gestured to the man with the receding hairline and facial scar. "Sloane, this is Gael O'Mahony, boss of the Sionnach Clan, and his son, Owen."

"It's a pleasure to meet you, Ms. Kavanaugh," Gael said, offering me his hand. I took it, feeling my palm slide against calloused skin.

"What does Sionnach mean?" I asked.

Gael looked pleased that I'd got the pronunciation right. "Fox," he replied. "In Gaelic. Do you know any Gaelic?"

I shook my head and slid my hand from his.

Finnan continued with the introductions. The balding redhead was Gannon Sweeney of Clan Fiach—his off-sider Seamus Hayes. Gannon leered at me, licking his lips as he dragged his heated gaze down my body. If it was possible to feel violated from a look, I was feeling that violation now.

"I'll take the whore after you're done with her, Quinn," he announced, reaching around to grab a handful of my ass. Noticing the bandage on my hand, he sneered, "Even if she is injured. I only need her mouth and pussy to be functional."

I was too stunned to react, but from my periphery, Grayson rose so abruptly from his seat that it tipped over backward, clattering to the tiled floor. I thought he was going to physically set the other man straight, until Finnan barked something harsh in Gaelic, causing Grayson to back down.

He then turned his ire to Gannon. "Back the fuck off, Sweeney. I know you like them young, but she's not for you."

Sweeney took a step back, his hands up in the universal sign of surrender. It was too bad the expression on his face didn't match.

Although I had a few choice words for the man, I chose

a different path. Gesturing to another man, I asked, "And who is this?"

Finnan squeezed my bicep. "Ryan Griffen. He's the boss of Iolair Clan."

"That's eagle, lass," Ryan said in a rasping baritone.

I looked back at Gannon, who was openly leering at me. "What does Fiach mean? Handsy Cradle-Snatching Asshole?"

Ryan hid his laugh with a cough and turned away to clear his throat.

Sweeney's mouth twisted into a snarl. "Be careful, lass," he warned in a low voice. "Or I'll add your ass to my list of fuck holes."

Another stream of Gaelic came out of Finnan as he glared at the other man. Sweeney's eyes were like ice as he stared at the Mac Tíre boss before finally backing down and looking away.

Finnan steered me toward the table.

That was when I noticed he had purposefully ignored the blonde woman and the older man she was with, who were already seated. Before I could find out why, the waiter appeared again, holding a tray with our drinks. He placed the bottle of Cristal and one champagne flute onto the table, then the whisky along with ten squat tumblers.

The waiter glanced up at the only other woman present. "Would the lady also like champagne?"

Glaring at me, she replied in a throaty rasp, "Whisky is more to my taste. I'll leave the champagne to the little girls."

Ignoring the comment, Finnan held out my chair for me,

and as I slid onto it, he squeezed my shoulders and leaned down to whisper in my ear, "You look ravishing tonight, my dear. Well done." He pressed a kiss to the side of my neck, taking in a deep breath as he buried his nose against my throat.

Grayson immediately poured himself a glass of the amber liquid. He swallowed it down in one gulp, then poured himself another.

"Are you going to fucking snub me, Quinn?" barked the man seated beside the blonde woman. "You've already sullied the fucking institution of our Conclave by bringing your Warlord and a whore, but you have the brass balls to *ignore* me and Aisling, too?"

"This is Mannix King, and his daughter, Aisling," Finnan replied in an off-hand tone as he took his seat. "Leader of the Bèar Clan."

My gaze shifted to Aisling, who was staring at me with her intelligent green eyes. A serpentine smile graced her lips. I dropped my eyes from her face, playing the meek, naïve woman they expected me to be. Let them underestimate me.

"And she's not a whore," Finnan added. "She's my future wife."

"*Wife?*" King repeated loudly, leaping up from his seat. He loomed over the table, but his fierce gaze was laser-focused on Finnan. Aisling seemed unruffled—the only reaction she gave was a slight raise of her naturally pale brows.

"What *the fuck* are you talking about, Quinn?"

My pulse roared in my ears as testosterone filled the air. I had no doubt that every single one of these men would commit violence without sparing a thought for where they were or what innocent people would be caught in the crossfire.

Without waiting for Finnan's reply, King said, "What about my Aisling? We had a deal!"

"What is he talking about?" Gael asked, looking between the men. "What deal?"

With a growl, Mannix replied, "He was betrothed to my daughter."

I watched Grayson's reaction to that, but his expression remained impassive. He'd either known about the arrangement, or his blank face was impressive. Turning my head, I stared at Finnan. His mouth was curved into a self-congratulatory smile.

"We did have an arrangement. The one I set up with her father was much more... advantageous." Finnan turned his green eyes to me. "She's younger. More beautiful, too. A much better decoration to have on my arm."

Aisling made a derisive sound down low in her throat and took a swig of her whisky.

"Decoration?" I hissed. "Did you just call me a decoration?"

"Sloane," Grayson said in warning.

Finnan turned his cold eyes to me. "Aye, lass, I did. Decorations don't speak. They remain silent in my presence."

I felt an unfriendly smile curve my painted lips. "I guess you just gave me permission to be the starfish in bed then. Fantastic. I won't have to fake my enjoyment or the orgasm you could *never* give me."

Some men around the table started to chuckle at what I'd said, but their laughter only threw fuel on the fire of Finnan's rage. His already cold eyes became arctic as he leaned in and hissed, "You'll do well to remember what I said to you before, Sloane."

Knowing how to play this game, I poured myself some champagne, watching the slender glass fill up with the yellow liquid. Taking the glass in my hand, I took a sip, then gulped down the rest of it in one swallow. After what I'd just done, I needed to do something with my mouth to stop it from working.

The waiter was there to refill it in an instant.

"I'm surprised you're here, Quinn," Sweeney said in a greasy voice. "I heard someone tried to take you and a number of your clan out last night."

Finnan's hand curled into a fist. "What do you know about it, Sweeney?"

"Nothing," he replied with a smug smile.

"You fucking bastard." Finnan rose from his seat, reaching inside his jacket as he did. Grayson shadowed him, standing, and pulling out his Glock.

Everyone at the table grew still as Sweeney and Seamus, Finnan and Grayson pointed guns at one another across the table.

Mannix stood, still outraged at the slight. "How the fuck could you do this to me, Quinn?"

Finnan pulled another gun from the small of his back and pointed it at the Bèar Clan leader. "Sit. The. Fuck. Down, Mannix."

"Father, sit down." Aisling tugged at her father's arm.

Mannix glared at Finnan but retook his seat. Finnan's attention went back to Sweeney. "You sure you didn't have anything to do with those car bombs?"

Grayson's gaze flickered to mine, then to the table. I nodded to show him I understood, scooting forward in my seat. He thought shit was going to hit the fan soon, and he wanted me out of the line of fire—literally.

Finnan snarled, "Fuck you, you arrogant, cock-sucking—"

Seamus tutted him. "Now, now, there's no need for name-calling."

"Shut it, gobshite," Grayson interjected with a snarl.

All the tiny hairs on my body raised at the impending threat.

"Or what, huh?" Seamus asked. "What are you going to do?"

Grayson lowered the muzzle of his gun, motioning with his hand for me to get down. Sliding from the edge of my seat, I disappeared under the table as gunfire erupted in the restaurant. The other patrons screamed, all scrambling to either take cover or flee. I looked back when I heard a curse.

Aisling was under the table with a hand on her father's back, holding him down. Our eyes met, and the malice I saw in them would've stripped the skin from my body.

"Bitch," she hissed, pulling her father out from under the table in a crouch and hustling him out.

Someone grabbed my arm, and I yanked away.

"Dammit, Sloane," Grayson barked. "I need to get you out of here. *Now.*" He hauled me out from under the table, keeping my head down with a hand on the back of my neck. "Toward the front door," he ordered.

I ran that way, trying not to react to the bullets hitting targets not even a foot from me. I reached the door first, only to realize another armed man was making his way inside.

"Fuck!" Grayson wheeled away, pulling me with him.

"Who was that?" I asked, covering my head with my hands.

"One of Sweeney's fucking sentinels," he growled. "This way."

He led me down the hallway toward the kitchen but cursed when another shooter came out of the swinging door. Grayson got off a couple of shots of his own before shoving me into the restroom.

"Lock the goddamn door!"

The door swung shut and I flipped the lock. With my breathing coming out in a rush, I retreated until my back hit the wall.

Then I waited.

And waited.

My mind churning with all the things that could be happening.

Was Grayson hurt? Had he been shot?

Then, in the lull of gunfire, someone started hammering on the door.

"Sloane, it's Torin."

I edged closer, placing my hand against the wood. "How do I know it's you?" I called back.

"You dragged me lingerie shopping with Fallon the other

day," he replied.

Anyone could've seen us. My father had taught me never to leave the scene of the abduction. Moving to another location reduced the chances of being found in time or meant they were ready to kill you somewhere else. Since I had no intention of getting killed today, I called back, "If it's really you, you'll know what flavor chips you bought me on the way to Galway that first time."

"Lass, we don't have time for this," he growled.

"Actually, I have all the time in the world. What flavor?"

"Prawn Cocktail. And they're Taytos," he corrected. "Open the door."

I did, revealing Torin standing in the doorway. His Glock was naked in his hand, and he had a smear of blood across his forehead. I felt my eyes widen.

"Grayson asked me to get you out of here."

"Where is he?"

"Handling it."

"Handling it?" I repeated incredulously.

"Aye, handling it." He glanced up the hall then back to me. "Come on." Torin urged. "We can go through the staff entrance at the end of this hall."

With one more backward glance, I followed Torin out the door.

There were three black Range Rovers in a row. With dark tinted windows, they waited in the alleyway behind the restaurant, smoke curling out from their exhausts as they idled.

Torin gestured to the middle vehicle.

And I got in.

21

GRAYSON

A SHOT SLAMMED INTO THE WALL BEHIND MY head, making me whip around to see where it had come from. Sweeney's men were crawling all over the place, the Fiach enforcers still streaming through the front door.

"You were supposed to be dead!" Sweeney yelled from behind his turned-over table. "You were supposed to be *fucking dead!*"

"The only one who's going to die is you, you bastard." Spittle flew from Finnan's lips as all that rage morphed his vocal cords. "Take this motherfucker out, Kent."

I turned to look at Finnan. "Boss?"

He jerked his head in the direction of Sweeney. "His clan was behind the fucking car bombing, and he dies for it."

"Finnan, think about this." Killing another clan boss was not something you did lightly. The repercussions would start a war.

Finnan rounded on me, his eyes burning with dark flame. "Kill. Him."

Seamus Hayes—Sweeney's Chief—who was taking cover behind another table, started yelling at his boss to run. Trying to get him to safety was his job.

"Finnan—" I decided to try one last time.

With an eerie calm, he said, "Finish him, or you're finished."

Letting out a breath, I brought up my Glock and peered around the corner of the table. Despite the direct order, I couldn't kill the other clan boss. I would become public enemy number one. I would be hunted by the Fiach's Reaper then tortured. I wasn't afraid of death, but when I thought about the risk of getting killed for my actions, my immediate instinct was to stop. Think. Fallon relied on me, and now I could add Sloane to that incredibly short list of the people I cared about.

I couldn't stomach the thought of leaving her to Finnan's mercy.

Or lack thereof.

Seamus put down covering fire while Sweeney backed away from the fight. I caught a glimpse of his face—his features twisted in a snarl—before he disappeared through the front door of the restaurant. I followed his movement with the muzzle of my gun, firing as soon as I got a clear shot. The window shattered, and the clan boss threw up his arm to protect himself from the razor-sharp glass, but did not slow down.

"Fuck," I muttered.

"Did you get him?" Finnan asked, peering through the gap in the table, not taking his eyes off Seamus and the remaining Fiach enforcers.

"No."

"Bastard! If I can't take out the clan boss, I'll take out his fucking second."

He took aim at Seamus and pulled the trigger. A spray of blood misted into the air, followed by a low moan.

"Fall back," yelled a pained voice. "Fall... back." An enforcer was dragging Seamus from the restaurant, his booted feet disappearing from between the jamb.

Outside, the wail of police sirens began to howl through the night.

"Finnan, we have to get you out of here. We don't own the cops in this town."

Reloading his gun, he asked, "Where's the girl?"

"I left her in the bathroom."

"Get her."

I hurried through the destruction, stepping over dead bodies, broken furniture, and glass. Hammering on the bathroom door, I called out for Sloane. "Lass? It's me."

There was no response.

Panic seized my shoulders.

I pushed against the door, swearing when I saw it was unlocked.

With my foot, I eased the door open, and when I didn't get shot at, I stepped into the tiled room. After checking the stalls, I realized Sloane was nowhere in sight.

It was empty.

It was goddamn *empty!*

I slammed my fist against the closest stall door, the hinges whining in protest.

Fuck.

Fuck.

FUCK!

Where the hell had she gone?

When I walked out of the restroom, Finnan was there. He looked over my shoulder. "Where the hell is she?"

I swallowed roughly, knowing the next word out of my mouth could be my last. "Gone."

"What the fuck do you mean *gone*? Where did she go?"

Shaking my head, I told him, "I don't know."

Brushing past me, Finnan's anger sparked against my skin. He looked around the restroom, then barked Sloane's name. When he came back out again, he ran a hand through his hair.

Outside, the sirens were getting closer.

"We have to go." Pulling out my phone, I tried to call Torin, but it went straight to voicemail. "Fuck!" So I called Trigger.

"Grayson?" he answered.

"We need to get out of here. *Now.*"

In the background, an engine roared to life. "I'm thirty seconds out."

"Pick us up in the back." I hung up and started toward the staff door that led out into the alleyway. The cops were closer now—maybe only another minute away at best—and we couldn't afford to be arrested.

Trigger pulled into the mouth of the alley thirty seconds later. Finnan took the back seat while I rode shotgun.

"Make us disappear," Finnan told Trigger, who put his foot down and got us the hell out of Dodge.

As we moved out of the city of Athlone and back toward Galway, tension gnawed at my gut. *Where in the hell was Sloane?*

"Call Torin again. See if he got her out."

I made the call, cursing when it went straight to voicemail. I tried again, the phone not even ringing once this time. I punched the dashboard. My breath was rattling out of my lungs, and when I turned my head, I could see Finnan staring at me through narrowed eyes.

I said, "No answer. What's the plan?" I hoped to God he had one because my idea to burn the country to the ground in order to find her had too many fucking moving parts.

"We return to Oranmore. Rally the clan. Sweeney fucking started a war."

"What about Sloane?"

He cocked his head to the side. "What about her?"

I licked my suddenly dry lips. "What if Torin didn't get her out?"

Finnan didn't have an answer for that, so we sat in silence on the way back to Galway. When we arrived at the compound, I left Finnan there and took the Rover back to my house. If shit was about to go south—if there was a war on the horizon—I needed to see my sister before that happened.

TWENTY MINUTES LATER, I WALKED IN THE DOOR OF my house to find Fallon pacing in the living room in front of the television. In one hand, she clutched a rosary and was reciting a Hail Mary prayer under her breath while her gaze remained fixed on the screen. She spun, though, when she heard the door slam behind me. As soon as she saw me, she threw herself into my arms, burying her face against my neck.

"I thought you were dead." Her words came out muffled.

I peered over her shoulder to see what they were reporting on the news—the firefight that had erupted.

"They said that a dozen people had been killed or injured. I thought it was you." Tears tracked down her face, and I wiped them away with my thumb. "I'm fine, Fallon, but I have to go. What happened tonight—" Fuck, I couldn't even finish that thought. I was likely to tear the whole world down if I did. With my jaw tight, I said, "I have to go."

As I stepped away to go to my bedroom to pack, she grabbed my arm.

"I'm afraid you won't come back," she admitted in a trembling voice. Her fingers tightened around my arm. "I'm afraid you won't come back, and I'll have no way of knowing if you're dead or alive."

"Fallon." I loosened her grip. "The clan would take care of you if I were gone."

More tears, and my heart was getting ripped from my chest with every single one.

"Maybe, but what the hell am I supposed to do without you?"

I wrapped her in my arms and kissed her forehead. "You're stronger than you think you are, Fallon. You know that. I know that. I believe you will *always* make the right decision when it comes to your sobriety."

Even though it killed me, I eased her away from me, gripping her by her upper arms to keep her from clinging to me again. "Fallon, I have to go."

"Where are you going?"

"We're preparing."

"Preparing? For what?"

As much as I didn't want to say it, I did, "War."

She drew in a large staccato breath, mentally steadying herself. When she looked up at me, there were tears in her eyes. "Just… be careful, okay?"

"Always," I replied fiercely. Grabbing the back of her neck, I pulled her close and kissed her forehead once more. Against her skin, I said, "You remember where I keep the money?" I tightened my grip until she nodded. "If I don't come back, take it and leave Ireland."

22

SLOANE

AS I WAS DRIVEN AWAY FROM THE CARNAGE of the Conclave, I lost all concept of where we were. Everything outside the windows was black, but I got the impression we were in the countryside—somewhere.

"How much farther?" I asked the driver in the dark confines of the car. I'd not met him before, but I had no doubt there were dozens of members of the Mac Tíre Clan that I'd never met.

The guy said nothing, and I wondered who the hell he was.

Torin had stayed behind at the restaurant, and I figured that had been under Grayson's orders—to get me out safely so he could return to the fight. In the warm darkness, I thought about Grayson. About whether he was okay. Had he gotten hurt? Had he been shot?

My heart squeezed in my chest, but I shook my head.

Worrying about the things that might have happened was pointless. It was all out of my control. Slipping off my shoes, I rubbed at my sore feet, hissing in a breath when I pressed too hard into the heel of my right foot. Strong and Silent in the front seat looked at me briefly before returning his attention to the road.

It seemed like forever had passed before the car began to slow. It turned into a long driveway, and I watched as a large building came into view as if it was rising from the earth. Spotlights flooded the sides of the building, bathing them in golden light that the rain cut through in sharp slashes. We passed through the stone wall and wrought iron gates that were guarded by men carrying rifles at their sides.

My stomach bottomed out. "What is this place? Another safe house?"

When the driver said nothing, I surreptitiously tried the handle of my door. It was locked from the outside. *Fuck.*

More lights had come on, so I could see that the building was made of red bricks that seemed to absorb the moonlight. A horseshoe-shaped driveway skirted a fountain in the middle of the courtyard. There also appeared to be two other buildings in the same style as the main house on either side of us. It looked like a manor house, but one that had been modernized with extra security and lighting.

The car was brought to a stop on the gravel drive, and another man I didn't know opened the door, holding an umbrella over him. His dark gaze traveled over me, and my instincts began to scream.

"Good evening, Ms. Kavanaugh," he said.

"Who are you?"

"You can call me Sam." He held out a hand to me. "Please step out of the car."

"I think I'll stay right here," I told him, my eyes darting to the side when another

man came into view—this one openly leering at me.

"I really must insist." He reached forward, taking me by the forearm. I let him pull me from the car, letting him think I wasn't going to resist.

The wind chose to howl across the open expanse of lawn, flinging needles of rain at my bare skin, and I shivered in my barely-there dress.

"Where's Grayson? Finnan?"

He smiled. "I expect they'll be along soon." His eyes darted down to my goose bumped skin. "We should get you inside."

The other man chuckled and licked his lips. Yeah, I just bet he wanted me inside. But it was clear that this was not a Mac Tíre safe house, and there wasn't a way in hell I was going to volunteer to serve myself up to whoever the fuck employed these men. My eyes darted to the side, eying the lawn that was being swallowed by the darkness. If I went inside, there was an incredibly good chance I wouldn't come back out again.

I looked back into Sam's face. "Fuck you, asshole." I took off running. The first few steps were torture on my bare feet. When I reached the lawn, I slipped on the slick grass. Landing on my knees with a huff, I risked a look over my shoulder to find Sam staring after me with an amused expression.

Well, fuck him and the horse he rode in on.

I took off again, the rain soaking me to the bone almost immediately. I pushed through a grove of trees, their rain-laden branches hanging low to the ground. Glancing left and right, I attempted to orient myself, but with the cloud covering the moon and stars, there was very little in the way of light.

Behind me, I heard someone grunt, then swear, and I took off again.

Up ahead, a large, solid object came into view. It spanned left and right for as far as I could see, and I guessed it was the perimeter wall. Skidding to a halt in front of it, I peered up. At least eight feet high. I could do this, though.

Retreating back a dozen feet, I set off at a run, launching myself at the brick wall. My fingers wrapped around the top edge, and I was about to pull myself up when something hard and warm wrapped around my ankle. I kicked, hearing an *oomph* of pain. Unbidden, a triumphant smile appeared on my lips as I prepared to go over the wall. I got my body up onto the top of a foot-thick brick wall and peered over the top. There was nothing but inky blackness on the other side, but I could hear the sound of running water somewhere down there.

I had to choose.

Dropping fuck knew how many feet down into a potentially icy body of water, in the dark, or surrendering to this unknown group of men. I'd never been very good at surrender. Swinging my legs around, I prepared to drop when someone's arms cinched around my waist from behind, and I was dragged backward.

"Got you now," a dark voice said, hauling me up and over

his shoulder.

Fuck, what was it with these Irish men and throwing terrified women over their shoulders?

With one arm banded around my thighs, he manhandled me back to the front of the building, where Sam was still standing with a smile on his face.

"Did she get far?"

"Almost over the wall," the man who was carrying me replied, grunting as he repositioned me. "Where do you want her? The cells?"

Fuck.

"No. There's a room prepared upstairs for her."

Sam shook out his umbrella and led the way inside. Looking under my ride's arm, I got an upside-down view of the world. A heavy, wooden door. An ancient hardwood floor covered in rugs. An oak staircase that took up most of the foyer space. Walls hung with tapestries and stuffed animal heads.

We walked up to the first floor, and I saw that the stairs ascended a little farther. On the first landing, Sam continued down a long hall where oversized portraits hung on plastered walls and a long runner cushioned his feet.

Eventually, we came to a stop, and Sam opened the door. The room beyond was empty except for a single, wrought-iron bed frame with a thin foam pad placed in the center.

When I was unceremoniously dumped onto the mattress, I whirled around and spat, "What the hell is this? Who are you?" But it was too late. The bedroom door was already closing—an ominous *click* punctuating the bolt sliding into the strike plate.

Calling on all the drills my father had made me do, I walked the perimeter of the room, looking for any loose floorboards, sections of wall, or anything I could use as a weapon. The bed—although made of iron—was literally bolted to the floor, and the springs had been welded to the frame.

Knowing there was no help coming—since nobody knew where the hell I was—I looked around the room again, trying to find either something I could use as a weapon or a way out. I re-checked the windows, contemplating shimmying out the damn things, but as I looked at the painted-over casement, I came to three realizations.

First, there was nothing I could wrap around my hand to protect it from the shattering glass.

Second, even if I did have something, the noise would draw the guards.

And third, the glass was infused with chicken wire. Even if I did break it, the thick chicken wire would prevent me from escaping out the window.

I shivered, and it had nothing to do with being dripping wet and more to do with being captured and held against my will for the second time in what I suspected was no more than a week.

Clearly, they wanted me alive. Otherwise, I would've been shot in the back of the Rover and my body dumped. The fact that they didn't, meant I was going to be used as a bargaining chip. And as a bargaining chip, they had to keep me alive, so no starvation for me. They would have to bring in food and water soon.

Death by hypothermia, however, was still a very real threat.

I noticed my breath hovering in front of my mouth with each exhalation, and I knew I had to get warmth back into my body somehow.

I glanced down at my bandaged palm, then at the welded bed spring—a plan formulating in my head.

Reaching down, I made sure to grab the gnarliest-looking spring—the one with the sharpest point—and yanked on it with my injured hand. Sure enough, the sharpened point dug into my already painful palm, amplifying the injury tenfold.

"Son of a bitch!" I yelled, pulling away. Fresh blood was already soaking into the gauze. Clenching my hand into a fist, I tried to stem the flow. With blood dripping from the bandage, I hammered on the door with my undamaged fist.

"Hey! I need a bandage in here!"

Silence.

"You want me to bleed out on the floor?" I yelled again.

More silence.

Infuriating silence.

"You need to keep me alive, so I suggest someone comes in here and helps."

The sound of a bolt being drawn back echoed through the room, and I retreated a few steps. The door opened, but instead of a guard, Aisling King entered the room.

The door remained open, a couple of guards standing at the ready.

Aisling's clear green eyes traveled around my pitiful, shivering, wet body before locking onto my bleeding hand. "Trying to win the sympathy vote?" She made a sound low in her throat that sounded like a scoff. "You won't be getting any sympathy from me." Without taking her eyes off me, she called, "James?"

One of the guards walked into the room. "Miss?" he asked. She scowled at him, and he quickly corrected, "Chief?"

"Bring the first aid kit. We can't have our guest bleeding to death, can we?"

James disappeared out the door without another word.

I called after him, "A blanket wouldn't go astray, either!" then returned my attention to Aisling. I licked my lips, wondering how in the hell this was going to play out. "Why am I here?"

One of her perfectly groomed brows rose. "Why?" Aisling asked in that throaty purr she had. As she approached, I caught a whiff of cigarettes and knew that the sexy timbre was from nicotine rather than genetics. "Because you're the thorn in my side. Everything was going according to plan until you showed up."

I nodded. "Finnan was supposed to marry you."

"And in doing so, merge our two great clans and create a power base for me to rule from."

I hated to break it to her, but if she married Finnan, she wouldn't be ruling over anything. "I think you're overestimating your appeal and Finnan's tolerance for anyone else's ego."

She narrowed her green eyes at me. "I don't overestimate anything. The deal had been made, and Finnan broke it."

My brows rose. "You think I *wanted* to be sold in a flesh auction then abducted and taken to another country? You think I'm here by choice?"

"I don't give a shit about what you want or what happened

to you," Aisling hissed, stepping a little closer. "All I care about is having the empire I was promised."

"Even if that means tying yourself to a man who promised I'd become the clan whore if I didn't toe the line?"

Aisling's eyes flared. "Finnan is ruthless."

"He's a psychopath, but I can see how you can confuse the two."

James came back into the room, first-aid kit in hand. He tried to hand it to Aisling, but she only stared at the proffered pouch with disdain.

"I'm not getting *her* blood on my dress," she told him.

I let James bandage my wound, which he did with the efficiency of an army medic who had to work quickly in the field. This wasn't a war zone, but it could so easily be.

Aisling watched the whole process, arms folded, mouth thinned.

"What's going to happen to me? You want me alive. Clearly."

"For now." She tapped her manicured fingers on her bare forearm. "But things change, Sloane, so very quickly."

When James began packing up the kit, he and Aisling left, locking the door behind them. Shoving the debris of the wound clean off the edge of the foam pad, I curled onto my side to try to conserve warmth and attempted to get some rest.

STILL CURLED IN A BALL, I WOKE UP SHIVERING, WITH my bare legs tucked up tight to my body. The room was freezing without any rugs on the wooden floor, but at least I had dried off a little. I was about to demand they turn up the heat when the bolt slid across, and the door opened. James was there again, carrying a tray of food. A bowl of what smelled like soup, a bottle of water, and a slice of bread. No utensils, lest I stab someone to death with them. I eyed James's body as he walked, pinpointing where his guns were stashed. He was packing some heat—one on his hip, two in the over-the-shoulder holster, and judging by the bulge on his left ankle, one also near his foot.

"Eat," he commanded when he put the tray down. "It'll warm you up."

Wrapping my arms around myself, I replied with chattering teeth, "I feel like I'll never be warm again. Can I at least get a blanket?"

"Sorry, no blanket. Chief's orders."

"So you won't kill me, but I can freeze to death?"

He gave me flat, expressionless eyes. Pointing at the soup, he said, "Eat."

James was almost at the door when I yelled, "What if it's poisoned?"

His shoulders hitched, and he came back, swiping up the bowl. Putting the rim to his mouth, he took a sip. Wiping the back of his hand over his mouth, he said, "Not poisoned. Eat."

He was out the door before I could think of another reason to get him to stay.

It only took me a minute of debating with myself as I watched the steam whisp off the hot soup before I gave in and ate. I dunked the bread, shoveling it into my mouth unceremoniously, still chewing even as I picked up the bowl and savored the heat that emanated from it. My hands were freezing, but as I brought the bowl to my lips and drank, the heat began to flow through me.

I knew it was short-lived, but I absorbed it all, if only for a moment. When I was done with the soup, I cracked open the bottle of water, pleased to see that it had been sealed. I drank half of it, wanting to conserve the rest if this was the only meal I was going to get.

As I stared at the water, it did make me wonder about using the bathroom. There was no bucket left behind to serve as a toilet, and the idea of squatting in the corner was less than palatable.

I was saved from finding out when James reappeared. He took in the empty soup bowl and nodded. "Bathroom?" he asked.

I clambered off the bed. "Yes."

He motioned for me to stand, then took me by the arm and led me out the door. The hallway was warmer than my prison cell had been, but it was still cold by my standards. James stopped at a door and pulled it open to reveal a modern toilet and sink.

"The door remains unlocked. Be quick."

I stepped into the small room and closed the door, relieving myself quickly before washing my hands. There wasn't even a mirror hung on the wall, which told me abduction could have been part of daily life here.

There was a sharp rapping. "Are you finished?" James asked through the door.

I opened it, letting him know how unhappy I was with

him. "Yeah, I'm done. You should really work on your people skills."

The stare he gave me was blank and scary AF. It unsettled me so much that I didn't even notice he was holding something. A hoodie.

Holding out his hand to me, he said, "Put this on."

I took what was offered, pulling the sweatshirt over my head. It belonged to a man, although no scent clung to the material. The hem hit my knees, which was an immediate improvement on my overall comfort level.

"Thank you," I mumbled.

He nodded imperceptibly, then took me by the arm once more and returned me to my room.

23

GRAYSON

SLOANE HAD BEEN MISSING FOR TWENTY-FOUR hours, and we were no fucking closer to finding out where she was. I still hadn't had word from Torin, and I only hoped that was because he was still with her—still protecting her as I knew he would.

We figured out he had to have been the one to get her out of the restaurant because there had been no sign of a struggle, and Sloane was smart enough not to move locations if she was under threat of abduction. She would've put up a fight otherwise.

But where the hell were they? Attempting to escape? Were they even still together, or had they been separated?

My agitation over losing her was catching. The whole clan—the whole compound— was like a powder keg getting ready to ignite. All it would take would be a single spark.

"Heard anything yet?" Finnan asked, stalking into the open-plan kitchen and pouring himself a drink of whisky.

I eyed the amber liquid as it cascaded down the sides of the tumbler. "Nothing."

"What about Gael and Ryan?"

Keir, who was pacing a hole into the rug, said, "Both the Sionnach and Iolair clans have heard nothing."

Finnan threw back what was in the tumbler before pouring himself another. "Mannix?"

"Haven't heard back," Shay replied. "Although, given how spectacularly you rejected his daughter, I don't suppose we can count on them as our allies anymore."

I turned when the sound of the giant front door opening and closing echoed through the room.

"It's just me," someone called from the darkness.

Torin. Thank fuck. He stepped into the room, looking at us all.

I took a step forward but stopped when Finnan placed his glass down with a thump and walked to the other man. For a long minute, he simply stared into Torin's dark eyes before pulling him into a tight embrace—hugging in a way I had never witnessed before. Lowering my weapon, I stared at the two men. With his hand still on Torin's shoulder, Finnan pulled his head back to stare at the other man.

His voice was low. "Are you okay?"

"Aye."

Finnan pressed their foreheads together briefly, then stalked back to get his whisky. He threw the remaining liquor back and leaned against the kitchen counter as if that display of emotion had never happened. When he spoke again, his voice was back to being cool and unaffected. "Where the fuck have you been?"

Torin swallowed audibly. "Making my way back here."

"Where were you?" I asked. "Where the fuck is Sloane?"

Torin's dark gaze flickered in my direction, and he swallowed roughly once more. My shoulders tightened. "I put her into the back of a Rover idling at the rear of the restaurant. I realized too late that—"

"Realized *what* too late?" I demanded, my anger beginning to boil over.

I could feel Finnan's suspicious eyes on me but ignored the scrutiny.

Torin hung his head. "It wasn't one of ours."

"You put Sloane into a car you didn't recognize?" My hands raked through my hair. "Fuck!"

"Who the hell did it belong to?" Finnan demanded, still eyeing me. Making a mental note to reel in my emotions, I bit back on every single one of my protective instincts.

"I don't know. It was dark. I couldn't see the driver."

"It was fucking clan Fiach," Finnan spat, hurling his whisky glass across the room. It smashed into the plaster wall, leaving an amber stain. "It had to be. We need to storm their fucking compound and get her back."

"Finnan," Keir said, trying to pump the brakes on his revenge train. "We don't even know if it was them." He gestured to Torin. "Torin even said he doesn't know who it belonged to."

Finnan rounded on his Chief, his nostrils flaring. "Then fucking *find* out where she is! I want that bitch back, and I want her back *now*. Nobody steals what belongs to me."

Scooping up his phone, he marched to the door. "I'll be at the fucking club blowing off some steam."

I looked at Keir for guidance, who jerked his head in Finnan's direction. "Do your job, Warlord."

24

SLOANE

THE NEXT TIME AISLING CAME TO ME, SHE WAS wearing a long, cream-colored couture dress—complete with a deep slit up the side—and heels encrusted with crystals. With her blonde hair perfectly styled, she peered down at me under a smokey eye, red lips, and an annoyed slant of her painted mouth. She was eyeing the hoodie with disdain like she found it personally offensive.

I sat up, having no idea how much time had passed. Shoving the hair from my face, I stared back at the blonde beauty, trying to figure out what we were going to fight about in this round.

"Who gave you that?" She flicked her fingers in the direction of the sweatshirt I was using as a makeshift whole-body blanket.

"James."

She shut her eyes and breathed in deeply through her

nose. When she opened them once more, her green gaze was cooler than before. "I've decided that I'm not going to let Finnan humiliate me like this. If he thinks he can simply replace me with you, I'll make it my life's purpose to punish him for it."

My mouth was suddenly dry. "What are you talking about?"

Lifting the hem of her dress, she pulled a Ruger LCP 380 from a micro garter on her thigh and pointed it at me. Aisling cocked her head to the side, her pale hair gliding from her shoulder. "Do you know how I became the Chief of this clan?"

My gaze darted between her and the gun. "No."

"Daddy didn't hand me this role. I had to work for it. Every. Damn. Day. Of my life. My father didn't believe I could or should rise in the ranks of the clan. But I did. I believe a woman can do anything she puts her mind to. And I enjoyed putting each and every man who ever said *I couldn't* in the ground."

"I get it. You're a man-hater." But what she'd said resonated so strongly with me. Did I want to rise through the ranks of my father's organization? No, but I wanted what Aisling had fought so hard for. Respect. Fear. Freedom to do what she wanted. Not be used as a pawn and sold to another man as a form of payment.

She arched a brow, tossing her wayward hair back over her shoulder. "I don't hate men, Sloane. They have their uses." She inched a step closer, tightening her grip on the weapon.

"There's just one thing I don't understand."

"And what's that?"

"You said you didn't want to marry Finnan."

"I don't. What I want from that man is power. The Mac Tíre clan is the epitome of power." She stepped closer, the muzzle of the gun finally touching my temple. I kept my eyes on her finger as she moved it off the trigger guard. I knew this gun—I had one myself back home—so I knew she had to use a fair amount of pressure to depress the trigger.

"It's a shame, really. In another life, we could've been friends, Sloane."

No. *No.* Fuck this. I wasn't going down like this.

"Any last words, Sloane Kavanaugh?" she asked.

I swallowed down on my dry throat. "Yeah," I croaked, shifting my weight forward. "How confident a fighter are you without a weapon?"

Before she could react, I slammed my fist into her solar plexus, compressing her diaphragm. Aisling stumbled away, clutching at the top of her stomach and sucking in vital oxygen. The gun fell from her hand, smacking into the iron bedframe and clattering to the floorboards.

I lunged for the weapon, scooping it up and turning the muzzle on Aisling. Her green eyes burned with hatred as her gaze flickered between the gun and my face. With her hand still clutching her midsection, she straightened as much as she could, meeting me face-on.

"You want to shoot me?" she asked, pressing her lips together in an attempt to hide her pain. "You want to end my life?" Aisling leaned forward, baring her teeth. "Do it, and my men will take you out before you can set foot outside this room."

"*Your* men, not your father's?"

Her face screwed up at the mention of Mannix King. "My father is weak," she spat. "Ever since his diagnosis and poor prognosis, he's been letting other clan leaders steamroll right over him. He's burying us, killing this once proud clan. But I will not sit idly by and watch it happen."

"That's why you want Finnan's influence." It all made sense now. "Joining with Finnan would provide the power you need to keep your clan alive."

She bared her teeth again. "Yes. My father worked for years to make this clan the most powerful in the country. But his own mortality is starting to influence everything he does. It's a weakness, and I will *not* have it in my clan. When my father is dead, I will rise up to claim what was once ours."

"Jesus. Does Finnan know you're this power-hungry?"

The smile she gave me made me shiver. "The leaders of these clans only see what they want to see. Women are weak. Men are strong. Women stay in the background. Men lead. Well, I'll be putting a stop to that as soon as possible."

I tightened my grip on the gun, finger loose on the trigger. I didn't want to kill her. I just wanted to get out of here. "What if I could promise you I'll never marry Finnan? Would you let me go?"

She arched a blonde brow and stared at me. Hard. "You'd give him up?"

"I never wanted him in the first place. My heart..." I paused, unable to say the next few words.

"Your heart?" she prompted, dropping her hand from her stomach. She stepped closer. "Your heart belongs to who?" A new smile spread across her lips. "Someone else.

Someone in the clan?" Another step until the muzzle of the Ruger was pressed to her chest. "You know, there are only three rules these men abide by." She counted them off on her fingers. "Don't talk to the police. Don't rat on another member. And the biggest is... don't get involved with the girlfriend, wife, or daughter of a member." Her cat-that-ate-the-canary smile widened, and she continued in a sing-song voice. "I'm willing to bet someone broke that the third rule. For you."

Fuck. I licked my top lip, suddenly anxious. "What's the punishment for breaking the rules?"

Aisling cocked her head to the side, her green eyes hyper-focused on me. "The member could be blacklisted. Beaten... or killed."

I felt my eyes widen.

I didn't know that.

In my father's organization, all of those were rules, too, but the harshest punishment was torture and exile. Death was never on the table.

"Are you going to pull the trigger, Sloane?" Aisling purred. "Are you going to shoot another woman who's struggling the same as you in this male-dominated world?"

Slowly, she reached out—as if to take the gun, thinking she had me—but I stepped away quickly.

With a huff, she said, "I'll find out which of Finnan's men has touched you. If he means anything to you, you'll try to save him." Aisling's gaze flickered from my face to something behind me, and as I spun, I was hit in the head...

And the world faded to black.

WHEN I CAME TO, I WAS TIED TO THE BED FRAME, and the hoodie was stripped from my body, so I was shivering in my dress once more. My head was pounding. Using my shoulder, I tried to push away whatever was running down the side of my face, my eyes widening when a bright red smear remained on my arm.

Fuck, I was bleeding. I didn't even know how long I'd been unconscious but judging by the flow of blood, it couldn't have been too long. Why couldn't I have just shot Aisling and been done with it? I had the chance, but she'd kept me talking—kept me distracted—so one of her men could come in and take me out.

Blood was flowing more quickly from the head wound now I was conscious. Pain throbbed in time with my pulse, and I knew I had to calm down. Rapid heart rates increased blood pressure, which would pump it straight out of my body. I needed to get myself under control, take a deep breath and figure out my next move.

There was a sound outside the door that drew my attention away from my pity party, and I stilled—straining to hear. The bolt on the door slid across, and I held my breath. Was it Aisling back to finish the job, or was she sending in one of her men to do her dirty work? Honestly, I would've taken her for the kind of woman who didn't mind getting her hands dirty. Maybe even relished the fact that she got her hands bloody every now and again.

So, when Torin slipped inside the room and shut the door, I couldn't speak for a full minute. His dark eyes traveled over me, unable to hide the wince when they landed on my head wound. "Christ, lass, are you okay?"

I blinked as he approached, noticing the gun tucked into the front of his slacks. "I don't know. I haven't seen my face yet."

He got a little closer to the wound, inspecting it without touching. "You might need stitches."

"What are you doing here?"

He stepped back, his eyes darting away before returning to my face. "I've come to rescue you."

Hope flared inside my chest, making me suddenly lightheaded. Or that could've been the blood loss. Who knew? "Grayson is here? The other sentinels?"

Running a hand through his hair, he looked down and shook his head. "Just me. They thought it was best if only I came in."

I pulled against the cable ties that were binding me to the bed frame. "Honestly, I don't care who came as long as I get out of here. Mind getting me out of these things?"

Torin reached into his back pocket and pulled out a folding knife. After severing the plastic ties, he repocketed the tool and helped me to stand. My legs gave out almost immediately. It was only Torin's arm around my waist that kept me from falling.

"Whatever you see and hear out there, Sloane, I just need you to trust me, okay?"

I stared at him for a heartbeat. "Okay?"

He nodded—resolute. "Let's go."

He helped me to the door and opened it. I braced for James or any number of Aisling's guards to stick their guns in our faces, but the hallway was empty.

"Where is everyone?" I asked.

"Shh. Keep quiet."

Torin started down the hallway—not moving cautiously like I thought he would—but moving with purpose. With authority. We were on the stairs, just hitting the first landing, when a group of men began their ascent from the ground floor.

"Just play along," Torin said softly, pulling the gun from the waistband of his pants and pressing it to my ribs. I jerked away, and it was only Torin's strong fingers wrapped around my upper arm that kept me from making a break for it.

"Where are you taking the prisoner?" one of the men asked. He had dark blond hair and muddy-brown eyes. He was built through the shoulders, had a thick neck and wide arms. He had meat shield written all over him.

"I've got orders to move her."

The other guard narrowed his eyes at Torin. "Who ordered you to do it?"

"Mannix."

The two men stepped aside immediately, and Torin jabbed the gun into my ribs a little harder to get me moving. I stared at him from the corner of my eye, trying to figure out how he was pulling this off. When we got to the bottom of the stairs, he shoved me toward the front door, which was being manned by another guard—the same one who had caught me outside.

"Where are you taking her?" he asked, eying me like he could see what was underneath my dress. "I was supposed to have a little fun with her later."

"Boss's order," Torin replied. "Ease down there, Jack." Pulling on my arm, Torin drew me through the door and into the back of a waiting Rover. As soon as the door was shut behind me, I stared at the front of the house, waiting for people to start pouring out the front door, guns drawn, yelling at us to stop.

It never happened, though.

Torin simply got into the front, gunned the engine, and drove off with me in the back.

"Do me a favor and not speak for a while," he told me in a hard voice. I looked at his eyes in the rearview mirror, then watched as he brought his finger to his mouth. Silence. Were they listening? Was the SUV bugged?

I nodded to show him I understood, and he passed a box of Kleenex back to me. Snapping half a dozen tissues free, I held them to my throbbing head. How in the hell had Torin been able to walk right out of there… unless… unless *he* was the rat everyone had been chasing? As much as I wanted to ask him—no, *demand* he tell me—I kept my lips shut and my breathing even.

Eventually, we pulled to a stop at a gas station. Torin slid the car into park, then turned around to look at me. He held his finger to his mouth once more, then started pulling out a small listening device that had been mounted under the driver's seat. Winding down the window, he threw it out then closed things up.

"Are you all right, lass?"

I nodded. "What the hell was that?"

He looked chagrinned. "Sorry about the gun."

"You're the fucking rat?"

Unease flickered in his dark eyes. "It's not what it looks like, lass."

"Then what does it look like?"

He blew out a breath, then turned his gaze to the gas pumps, where people were going about their business.

"I don't know how to explain it."

"Well, you should try. How in the hell did we just walk out of that compound? How did you get in? Just *how*?"

Turning in his seat, he stared at me, not speaking until I met his eye. "I need you to trust me, lass."

"Trust you?"

"Aye. You're not safe yet. Once I have you back to Finnan, I'll tell him everything."

I was in a predicament here. On the one hand, I had to trust him. I had to trust that he would take me back to Finnan and the Mac Tíre clan. He was my only hope at this point. On the other hand, if he *was* the rat, what would stop him from turning around and taking me back to the Bèar Clan at the drop of a hat?

"Please, Sloane. Don't make me threaten ya with telling Finnan about you and Grayson. You know what will happen to him if he finds out you've been fucking behind his back."

I kept my face neutral, my breathing even. "I don't know what you're talking about."

His expression faltered, slipping into sadness. He shook his head. "Aye, you do. I'll keep your secret, but I need you to keep mine just a little longer. Just until I can explain everything to Finnan."

My options were cut down to two. I couldn't let Grayson be killed for our relationship—if that's what it even was—

and if Torin told the clan boss about it, I had no doubt that Finnan would pull the trigger.

I knew Torin's secret, and in order to keep my silence, he held Grayson's life in his hands.

I blew out a breath. "Okay."

His brows rose. "Okay? You'll keep my secret, and I'll keep yours?"

"Yes."

He studied my face for a while longer before nodding. "Your word is your bond, Sloane, and I'll be holding you to it."

"Same for you, Torin." I folded my arms to stave off the chill that was creeping into the car.

"I need to take a piss. Wait here, okay?"

"Sure."

He got out of the car, locking the door behind him. I waited until he was out of sight before climbing into the front passenger seat. Opening the glove compartment, I rooted around in there looking for something—anything—that I could use as a weapon. When all I could find were receipts and a log book, I tried the center console.

"Bingo," I murmured after I lifted a packet of baby wipes and found a Glock sitting there. It was loaded, too. I was about to close the lid on the console when a small, black leather-bound book that had been under the gun caught my eye. It was probably half the size of a piece of letter paper, the initials MK embossed in gold on the front.

Risking a glance out the window, I couldn't see Torin yet, so I pulled out the book and took a look.

Holy shit.

I leafed through a few more pages, reading the lines of numbers and descriptions.

This was the money book for the Bèar clan. It was a ledger of every single transaction that came through the clan, including some that were highlighted, and the words *Mac Tíre consignment* were underlined.

Another look out the window and I saw Torin emerge from the shop. Scrambling into the back, I sat on the book and tucked the gun into the space between my spine and the seat at the small of my back. With a start, I realized the console hatch was still open, so I lifted up my foot and kicked it shut.

Pulling open the driver's side door, he stuck his head in and said, "I got you a hoodie, lass, and a bag of those prawn cocktail Taytos you like."

He handed back the hoodie first, waiting for me to put it on, then handed me the snack.

"Thanks," I said, breaking open the bag and shoveling some chips into my mouth. I was starving.

His eyes shifted to my head wound. "It looks like the bleeding has stopped. That's good. Maybe no need for stitches after all."

"Fingers crossed," I said.

Torin settled into the seat and turned the engine over. Slipping the gun and book into the front pocket of the hoodie, I waited for Torin to peel out of the gas station and get us back onto the road before I released the breath I'd been holding.

25

GRAYSON

FINNAN SAT AT ONE OF THE BANQUET TABLES IN the back, kicking his legs out in front of him. When the girls had seen him arrive, they'd all but flocked to him, fighting each other to be the one who gave him a lap dance first. I hated the thought that Sloane was going to have to put up with this shite. Finnan had no intention of remaining faithful to his wife.

Up on the W-shaped stage, three girls were working their respective poles stationed on each of the arms, grinding their way to bigger tips. The men surrounding them all watched with greed and lust gleaming in their eyes. It was true there was a time when I'd enjoyed being here, but ever since finding Sloane, the whole idea of getting blow jobs on tap didn't seem all that appealing. I really only wanted one woman's lips wrapped around my dick, and they belonged to Sloane.

Finnan raised his hand to get my attention.

I walked to him. "Sir?"

"I want Rhapsody over here. She can put her lips to good use."

I chewed the inside of my cheek, and I searched for the woman who—knowingly or unknowingly—was aware of my transgression. I found her talking to another patron. Her arms were around his neck, pushing her breasts into his chest as she said something in his ear. The man laughed, then sat a little straighter as I approached.

"Rhapsody, your services are needed," I told her.

She narrowed her blue eyes at me, clearly remembering our last discussion. "No."

"For fuck's sake, Rhapsody, Finnan's requested you."

Her eyes lit up at that statement. She scooted off the other man's dick and bounded over to Finnan. She slid into his lap, laying one hand over his shoulder while the other ran down his chest.

She turned her malicious eyes to me. "Going to join us, Grayson? I know you like to share women."

"Not tonight," I bit back, shooting her a warning look. The bitch had either forgotten or was choosing to play with me.

She shrugged, then started to work her hips on Finnan—gyrating and rubbing her cunt all over him. I turned around, unable to watch the show. Besides, I had no reason to. I had to look out for other threats. Rhapsody may have been a possessive cunt, but she wasn't a threat to Finnan's life.

The song continued on, and I surreptitiously kept tabs on them in the mirrored wall as the woman worked Finnan's dick into a frenzy. He wrapped his hands around her waist, bouncing her against his cock, and making his head kick back. Would he continue to use these women once Sloane was in his bed? It would be a goddamn fucking shame if he did.

I turned away in disgust.

Rhapsody laughed, then gasped suddenly, and I turned to find Finnan with his hand wrapped around her throat.

"What did you say?" he hissed, staring at the woman whose lips were moving wordlessly as she tried to draw breath.

She smacked at his hands ineffectually, trying to pry his fingers off. I took a step forward but drew to a stop when he turned those cold eyes on me.

He loosened his grip enough for her to speak. "I saw them together," she gasped.

Dread filled my chest, weighing it down—making it hard to breathe.

"Where? When?"

"At a club in Galway." She clawed at his fingers again, but he wasn't letting go. He turned his feral gaze to me.

"Is what she's saying true? Have you been touching things that don't belong to you, Grayson?"

Fuck, fuck, *fuck!* "Boss," I started, stepping back when he let Rhapsody go and stood at the same time. The stripper tumbled to the floor, hitting her head on the edge of the table as she fell. I knew it was stupid to take my eyes off him, but I had for a second, and when I looked back up, he had his gun aimed at my head.

"Start talking."

I put my hands up in front of me. "Not here."

He stepped closer. "You don't get to tell me where we talk this shite out. Start. Fucking. *Talking!*" His voice had risen to a fever pitch, and I sensed everyone in the club staring.

"This is bad for business," I said.

"Fuck the business."

"Finnan, he's right."

I turned my head to see Mary walking toward us. "Finnan, take this shite back to the compound. If what the whore said is true, you can take your pound of flesh out of his arse." She pinned him with a hard look. "But *not* here. *Not* in our place of business."

Finnan lowered his weapon in deference to Mary's instructions, stretching his neck out as he did. "We settle this at the compound," he seethed, walking past me. I turned to follow him but stopped when I caught Rhapsody's savage smile.

"Happy now?" I spat, turning away.

"I'll only be happy when your little girlfriend is punished," she yelled back. "You were mine, Grayson Kent. Nobody else's!"

Mary took me by the shoulder and spoke low, "If this is true, Kent, you better pray Finnan is in a merciful mood."

I stared after where my clan boss had disappeared, already knowing that mercy wasn't going to be in the cards for me tonight.

Outside, I got into the Rover and drove Finnan back to the compound, seriously contemplating just driving us into a ditch. At least my death would be quick. When I pulled into the driveway at Oranmore, Finnan got out before the car could come to a complete stop and marched into the house. Shutting off the engine, I followed him in, staring at Quillen, Shay, Caolan, and Orin's faces, as well as a dozen sentinels who had gathered.

Mary must've called ahead to warn them shit was going down.

Furniture had been cleared in the center of the room, forming a circle that the other men surrounded. Finnan was going to take his pound of flesh physically, which I supposed was better than being straight up introduced to a bullet.

Finnan took off his jacket and started unbuttoning his shirt, shrugging it off his shoulders. I did the same, peeling off my button-down and exposing the room to my scar and tattoos. Finnan's eyes dropped to the raised skin on the front of my shoulder, the one I had gotten in defense of his life.

"How could you have done that to me?" he asked, anger igniting his words. "You, who were my most loyal soldier. You took a fucking bullet for me. My trust isn't given lightly, Grayson, and you've gone and shit on it because of a fucking woman!"

I had protected his body—almost costing me my life. "Let me explain."

"There's nothing to explain!" he roared. "You've been fucking my fiancée. How long has it been going on?"

I felt more than saw the ripple of surprise that went through the other members of the clan.

"Finnan—"

"Did you seduce her, or did the whore come to you of

her own accord? Did she see that you were the weak link…
the chink in my armor? I fucking trusted you, Grayson. I
trusted you with Sloane's life, and you went and fucked her?"

I remained quiet. There wasn't a damn thing I could say
that would make Finnan stop rampaging. Yes, I had fucked
Sloane, but it'd had nothing to do with him. It had been
because I was obsessed with her. All that time watching her,
learning her… I *knew* her. I knew her in ways Finnan never
could understand nor begin to understand.

He brought his hands up in front of him, but I shook my
head. I swore to protect Finnan with my life. "No."

"Fight me!" he yelled. "Fight me like a fucking man."

"No."

His mouth twisted into an irritated snarl. "Fine." He
cocked his fist back and hit me in the face. I spun—unable
to stop the momentum—and landed on the floor, my hands
planted in an almost push-up position. Finnan was stronger
than he looked—something I knew from experience when
we sparred. My jaw felt as if a truck had run straight into
it. Hinging it back and forth, I stood up for the next blow.

Finnan looked murderous. His green eyes burned with a
hatred I had never witnessed before. Impatiently, he shoved
some of his dark hair from his face then bared his teeth.
"You dumb fuck."

This strike came at my stomach, shoving the air violently
from my body. I fell to my knees, barely recognizing the
pain of the *crack* that had heralded their meeting with the
tile. Hunched over, I gasped in air, but never got enough.

Because I was bent over, I never saw his foot coming until
it was too late. Blood sprayed in an arc from my nose, the

break feeling far worse than any other I'd sustained before. Toppling over to the side, I curled in on myself, trying to protect my vital organs as my boss began to beat me to death.

Blood was dripping onto the tile beneath me, making me slide a little each time Finnan exerted any force. I curled tighter still, tucking my head down farther, bringing my forearms in close to my torso, and bending my legs. He wailed on me for so long that I think I blacked out because when I came to, a hushed silence had fallen over the room.

Bringing up my head, I turned and looked through my one good eye to see Finnan with his gun pointed at me. His breathing was hard, his nostrils flaring from the effort. Blood covered his knuckles and bare chest.

I knew I deserved this, but the idea of leaving Sloane behind, knowing what Finnan would do to her for her part in this, made me want to fight. For her. For us. To live with the woman I loved.

The woman I... *loved?*

How in the fuck hadn't I seen it before now?

I couldn't leave Sloane like this—stuck in this life without any options. Even if I couldn't have her, I had to be there to protect her in whatever capacity I had.

Opening my mouth, I licked my lips—tasting blood—then croaked, "I'm calling in... my life... debt."

"No," he bit out, his fingers tightening on the grip of the gun. Although he was angry now, there was no way he could forget the last time I was this bloody at his feet. Time slowed—dwindled down to just the two of us staring at one another over the muzzle of a gun. "No," he repeated.

"Finnan," Keir said, breaking the intensity of our stare. "Once the debt is called in, you have to honor it."

Finnan turned his head to stare at the Chief of the Mac Tíre clan and bared his teeth. "He touched what belonged to me. For that, he deserves to die."

"Don't lose your Warlord, your *brother in arms*... over this," Keir pleaded. "Over a fucking piece of arse?"

"Fuck you," he seethed before turning his feral eyes to me. His jaw worked violently as he stared at my face. "I accept the life debt. But you need to know that she fucking belongs to *me*, and she always will whether she's the clan's whore, or just my own."

I wanted to pick up a gun and make him eat a bullet for coveting what was mine—clan boss or not—but I had to remember this was my punishment for stealing what was rightfully his. If it meant that I could live—even without Sloane—then I would take it. I would watch over her from a distance.

"Agreed," I rasped, coughing and spitting out blood.

Finnan put the weapon up. "Fuck!" He stalked away, only to return a moment later. "I can't have you as my Warlord anymore. I can't fucking *trust* you."

I nodded.

"From now on, you're a fucking sentinel. You can do the grunt work until I can trust you again... *if* I can trust you again."

He eyed me like I was dog shit on the bottom of his shoe before stalking off, and I attempted to get upright. With a grunt, I fell backward. From the pain radiating out near my ribcage, I suspected some bones had been broken. Better broken ribs than a bullet through the skull. Deciding to lay still for a moment, I shut my eyes and breathed as shallowly as I could to mitigate against the pain.

26

SLOANE

THE SCENT OF BLOOD WAS THICK IN THE AIR. I knew it was blood before we'd even entered the living room. What we walked into, though, made my stomach clench tight.

Grayson was sprawled on the floor, bloody—broken. One eye was swollen shut. My world came to a halt as I stared at him, wondering how bad the injuries were. Wondering whether he would be able to get back up again. Whether he was still alive.

The deepest chasm opened up inside my chest at that last thought. What if his heart had simply given up, and I never had the chance to tell him how I felt?

"Where the fuck have you been?" Finnan's question jarred me from my thoughts.

I darted my eyes to Torin then back again. "Aisling King had me."

"What did that bitch want?"

"She said she wasn't going to let you break the engagement."

He stared at me for a moment before eventually saying, "She said that, huh?"

I nodded.

"That's the reason she kidnapped you? To get you out of the way?"

My eyes strayed in Grayson's direction until Finnan grabbed me by the upper arm, shaking me. Snarling. "Don't fucking look at him!"

Stomach clenching tight, I swallowed down on my tight throat. Did he know about us? And if he did, had Grayson already received his punishment? Had he already been killed? No, his finger twitched, his eye flickering open. Our gazes locking. Hope surged.

"Don't kill him," I whispered. "Finnan, I'm *begging* you. Don't kill him."

His mouth curved into a sneer that made the back of my neck prickle. "You don't want me to kill him?" He looked between Grayson and me—Grayson trying to communicate something to me—although what that was, I had no idea. "Look at me when I'm talking to you." Grabbing my chin, he yanked my face back around to his, forcing me to look into his eyes. "What would you do to save his life?"

"Anything." The word fell from my lips before I'd even given it permission. But as I stared at the malice in Finnan's eyes, I meant it.

"Anything, huh?" Licking his lips, his heated gaze tracked

down my body, touching every intimate part of me. "What about giving yourself to me every night? Would you do that?"

Grayson made a small noise of protest, and I pulled from Finnan's grip for a second to see the defiance in his blue eyes and a slight shake of his head. He didn't want to share me, but he needn't have worried. I had a better plan.

"Look at me!" Finnan barked. "Not him. He's a fucking disgrace to the clan."

My heart began to thud violently against my ribs. "What do you mean?"

He threw his head back and laughed. The sound wasn't joyful. Instead, it was edged with anger. With scorn. "I know all about you two. I know that instead of leaving you alone, he pursued you. I know that you let him touch you. I bet you did it just to screw him over. You knew what would happen to him if he was caught."

I raised my chin in defiance, unwilling to answer the charges he was bringing against me. Mostly because I was ashamed that I hadn't had the fucking willpower to say no to him. I wanted Grayson Kent. Roughly. Brutally. Completely. "I can give you something better than his life."

Finnan's green eyes darkened to a deep forest leaf at midnight. "And what would be better than killing the man who defiled my fiancée every time my back was turned?"

I gripped the gun still hidden in the front pocket of the hoodie, my fingertips brushing past the barrel to touch the book. "The rat." Wrapping my palm around the gun, I brought it up and aimed it at the back of Torin's head. He immediately stiffened.

Every other clan member in the room pulled out their own Glock and trained it on me. My heart knocked more frantically against my ribs in an attempt to get out, but I held my nerve. Meeting each man's eyes for a second, I reset my attention on the biggest threat.

Finnan.

His nostrils flared as he followed the line of my arm to the end of the muzzle pressed hard against Torin's head. "What the fuck do you think you're doing?"

"What I have to." I was breathing heavily through my mouth as I shoved the gun in tighter to Torin's skull and said, "He's the rat. He rescued me from the bathroom the night of the shoot-out only to escort me to one of Mannix's Rovers waiting out back. He walked me out of the Bèar clan's compound not more than two hours ago without any challenge. They know who he is. They *trust* him."

It felt as if the whole room held its breath. The silence echoed, making my pounding pulse somehow louder in my ear.

"Finnan," Torin said softly, not moving. "She's lying."

"I can prove it." Reaching down, I stopped when the dozen guns that were trained on me were chambered—a round readied. "I'm just getting something out of my pocket."

"Caolan," Finnan called, his eyes still on Torin. "Get it."

"No. I get it, or I blow his brains out." I shoved the gun in hard, making Torin suck in a hissed breath.

"Caolan!" Finnan barked, halting the man with nothing more than his name. "Reach for it carefully, lass. One twitch and my clan will open fire, then fuck your lifeless body into oblivion."

Dipping my chin, I acknowledged his warning and slowly reached for the book. I took it out, holding it up so Finnan could see the embossed letters on the front.

He didn't look impressed. "What the fuck is that supposed to be?"

My lips and mouth were dry when I drew in a deep breath through my nose and said, "The Bèar clan's money book." I watched the reaction of everyone in the room. "Mannix King's ledger. It has everything in here, including payments to Torin for his information about your hijacked shipments. Every single one of the deals he made. Every single deal the Mac Tíre clan had that was targeted."

"She's fucking lying, Finnan," Torin said, desperation giving his words volume. "Shoot the bitch."

"I'm not lying. Why would I fucking lie about this?"

Finnan jerked his chin in Grayson's direction. "To save his life."

He was right. I would do anything to save Grayson, but that same spark of defiance was back in his eyes, making me hesitate.

"Give me the book." Finnan held out his hand for it.

"No."

"Aye, Sloane. You will give me the book."

I shook my head vigorously. There was no way I was giving up my only bargaining chip. "The only way I'll give it to you is if you agree to break the engagement. To let me go. To let me leave this room unhurt and to leave me alone forever."

Well, that certainly surprised him. "You have one chance, and instead of saving that cocksucker bleeding on the floor, you save yourself?" He appraised me carefully, looking… pleased with my decision. "You're ruthless."

I gave him a saccharine smile. "In more ways than one."

"Perhaps you would've made a better wife than I'd given you credit for."

Grayson caught my attention, nodding this time—the barest movement of his head. "The book for my freedom. Do you swear it?"

His eyes darted to Torin, who had started to sweat. He knew his luck had just run out.

"Aye, Sloane," Finnan eventually said. "We have a deal." He reached for the book, but I pulled it out of reach.

"You all heard it." I spoke loudly, making sure every clan member was listening. "A man is nothing without his word. Do you all agree?"

Everyone nodded.

"And Finnan agreed to break the marriage contract and set me free."

A chorus of "ayes" went up, and I had to trust that the Irish mafia, like my father's American-Irish, meant their word was their bond.

When I lowered the gun, I was grateful. My hand had started to cramp, and a shaking hand would've given me away. Finnan snatched the book from my hand, leafing through it immediately.

"Motherfucker. Mother-cocksucking-*fucker*!" He turned to Torin. "You'd better start talking, gobshite."

"Finnan, please." He backed away a few paces, and I

stepped to the side, slumping against the nearest wall. The adrenaline that had been zinging through my system had waned, and I was left feeling weak and lightheaded. I had just talked my way out of this clusterfuck of a marriage arrangement, but I hadn't been able to save Grayson.

When I felt eyes on me, I glanced over to find him staring. He blinked his eye once—slowly—then shifted his attention back to the two men in the center of the room.

"Why?" Finnan growled, pulling out his gun and holding it to the other man's head. "*Why*, you cocksucking bastard? Why would you do this to the clan? Why would you do this to *me*?"

"I had no choice."

"No choice? You had no fucking loyalty to the clan?"

"You don't understand." He backed up another step, and Finnan followed him. His expression was murderous, but underneath the anger was hurt. Betrayal.

"I understand that my own brother chose to fuck me up."

Brother?

I felt the word hang in the air, then watched it ripple through everyone else in the room. Nobody else had known. Not even Grayson, whose one functional eye had widened in disbelief.

"Finnan, what do you mean, brother?" Caolan asked.

"*Half*-brother," Torin supplied, placing emphasis on the first word. "We shared the same father. My mother was his whore."

"You've been more than a half-brother to me, and you damn-well know it," snarled Finnan. "So start fucking talking, or I *will* end your life, half-brother or not."

"I can't."

Finnan stepped closer still, herding Torin against the wall. The muzzle of the gun was pressed so hard to his temple that it dimpled the skin—mottling it. "Are you trying to protect that *fuck*, Mannix King? Are you his bitch now?" His finger moved to the trigger.

"Please, Finnan, believe me when I say I didn't want this. I didn't want any of this, but I got in too deep and… and… they threatened to hurt… her." He pressed his lips together.

"Threatened *who?*" This question came from Quillen. "Who did they threaten?"

Finnan's arm began to shake, and he pulled back, dropping it to his side. Stepping away, his eyes were on the floor, his expression lost.

"Finnan," Keir called, stepping up. "Finnan, you can't let this slide. He's our fucking *rat*. He's been telling a rival clan when things are going down, so our shipments and consignments are taken before we can get there. He's fucked with the clan, are you're going to let him go?" The Chief was yelling now, his anger flaring to life.

There was a communion between the pair then—some unspoken conversation. Eventually, Torin said, "If I didn't do what they wanted, they were going to go after her to get the money I owed."

It looked as if the words hurt Finnan more than the betrayal. He stared sightlessly for a moment before telling Keir, "Take him away."

Keir nodded, then jerked his chin at Caolan, who helped haul Torin from the room.

The rest of the clan started talking among themselves while Orin and Quillen went to Finnan. They spoke in hushed voices, and I saw this as my chance to escape with Grayson.

Using the distraction, I hauled Grayson onto his feet and helped him out the door. Leaning his substantial body weight against me, I beelined to the car Torin had escaped with and propped Grayson against the rear quarter panel to open the passenger door. Once he was inside, I ran around to the driver's side and got in, having no idea where we were going to go.

Only knowing that I was free.

That *we* were free.

27

GRAYSON

"FUCK." HOLDING OUT MY HANDS, I TRIED TO STOP being thrown around the backseat of the car while Sloane was behind the wheel, but since I wasn't buckled in, it was a losing battle.

"Slow down, lass," I told her, sucking in a hissed breath as my ribs started screaming at me.

I caught a glimpse of her wide gray eyes as she glanced over her shoulder. "Sorry, but there's no fucking way I'm slowing down right now."

"Nobody's chasing us. You can slow down."

This time it was an incredulous look from the rearview mirror. "What?"

Drawing in a shallow inhale through my nose, I repeated myself, adding, "Finnan isn't going to kill me. We made a deal."

Shaking her head, she muttered something under her

breath.

Prompting her, I asked, "What was that?"

"What kind of deal, Grayson? One where you're indebted to him for the rest of your life? One where you promised to stay away from me? One where he can ask you to kill me at any time?"

A small smile cracked my lips for the first time since she was abducted. Sloane was concerned for my life, though, and that deserved a smile. "Remember I told you I got shot?"

She nodded.

"I got shot trying to protect Finnan's life." Turning my head, I looked out the rain-streaked window. "We were walking to a meet when a sniper took out Finnan's father, Kellen." I ran a hand over my face, wincing when I forgot that I'd been beaten so severely. The throb that had disappeared when I'd seen Sloane came back with a vengeance. "I was only a caddie at the time, but when I saw Kellen go down, I knew Finnan would be the next target. So, I stood in front of him just as the crack of a rifle echoed through the air. I was hit in the shoulder."

My tongue was thick as I remembered that day again. "The event itself is hazy after that. It was snatched conversations here and there. A ride to the hospital. Being rushed down a white hallway with bright fluorescent lighting. Waking up hooked to tubes and wires and machines afterward. But there was one thing I remember with absolute clarity."

"What was that?"

"Finnan told me he owed me a life for saving his."

"That explains the look in your eyes. It was like you were

telling me to be careful... to think about what I was asking for."

"Aye, lass. I was already safe. If you had told Finnan you wanted to save me instead, you would've condemned yourself to a lifetime of mistreatment and pain."

She let out a shuddering breath, slowing the car as she took an off-ramp. I had a brief moment to marvel at her. She was heading back to Galway.

"How do you know where you're going?"

"My father trained me to remember routes and directions in the likely event I was kidnapped." Humor danced in her eyes. "I'm heading back to my apartment, or what's left of my apartment, I guess, unless you have another destination in mind?"

I did. I gave her the directions to get to Fallon and my house. When she pulled up, she got out of the car immediately and opened the back door. Her eyes scanned me from head to toe—looking for any other injuries she may have missed the first time—before she helped me sit, then swung my legs out. They took my weight, but my ribs were still hurting like a sonofabitch, and my breathing was ragged by the time we reached the door.

Fallon opened it before I could, her blue eyes wide as she took me in. "Jesus, Grayson." She helped Sloane get me inside. "On the couch," she commanded, her training to become a nurse taking over.

From my recumbent position, I watched as she hurried off, returning a moment later with a first-aid kit and an expression that let me know she hated seeing me like this. I had to admit it was humbling. I hadn't been on the receiving end of a beating for nearly a decade.

Fallon opened the kit, selecting gauze and saline to start the patch job. "Where does it hurt?"

"Mostly the right side of my body."

"Dizzy? Spotting vision or hearing?"

"Just a pounding headache."

She pursed her lips. "What about breathing?"

"Glad to be doing it still."

She palpated my ribs, where the skin was starting to go purple with bruising. "Tender?"

I sucked in a hiss and nodded. My eyes flickered to Sloane, where she stood against the wall, her fingers winding together as she watched. I kept my gaze locked on her while my sister doctored the wounds on my face, only breaking contact when Fallon had to reposition herself to cut off my t-shirt.

My sister checked every remaining wound and contusion, bruise, and lump, finally declaring that I'd live, even with what she suspected were two cracked ribs. "If you start pissing blood, I need to know," she said, packing away all the excess supplies and zipping the first aid kit shut. "No messing around either. Blood equals internal injuries, and I'm not fucking equipped to treat that at home."

"Okay." Christ, my mouth was dry.

"Gray, I'm serious." She turned away to wipe the tears she didn't want me to see from her face. "I can't lose you as well."

I touched her shoulder. "I promise, Filly."

The tears grew larger at the sound of her childhood nickname. With one final squeeze on my shoulder, she rose from her crouched position beside the couch and cleared away all the bloody gauze and ripped open packets.

Sloane unfolded her arms and perched on the side of the couch beside me. Catching a lock of her hair, I twisted it around my finger—ignoring the goddamned pain bitching at me. She was too beautiful not to touch, and she caressed what little part of my face that wasn't throbbing in time to my heart, and I leaned into it. I'd not allowed myself any comfort for so long. I always had to be the strong one, the one who protected the people I loved. Comfort was a foreign concept, but I wanted that comfort from Sloane.

I licked my dry lips, and she stood abruptly. "I'll go get you some water."

She was back a few moments later, and she helped lift my head to take a small sip from the bottle she'd gotten out of the fridge. When I'd had my fill, she settled me back into position and screwed on the cap.

"Fallon is pretty amazing," she said.

"Aye, she is."

"Quick to react. Didn't waste time asking questions that didn't matter." She straightened her spine a little, rolling back her shoulders. Taking my hand in hers, she let me peek behind her strong façade, allowing me to see how much this all had upset her. "Seeing you on the floor, surrounded by blood…" Shaking her head, she drew in a deep breath and let it out. "When I first walked in, I… I thought you were dead. I thought you were dead, and I was too late." She dropped her head into her hands like admitting that to me was somehow embarrassing.

I stroked her hair. "Sloane. Baby…"

"I don't know when it happened or why, but..." She finally looked up at me. "Somehow, I've fallen in love with you, Grayson."

My aching heart soared. "You love me?"

An earnest nod. "Yes."

The weight that had been sitting on my chest was suddenly lighter. "Thank Christ, lass, because I love you, too. I've loved you since the first day I laid eyes on you." I marveled at my woman. She was brave. Resourceful. Stalwart. Fucking stubborn. But she was mine. "Lay with me?" I asked her, my voice raspy.

She eyed my injuries with growing trepidation. "I don't want to hurt you."

"Every minute you're not pressed against me is hurting me."

Carefully maneuvering herself into position, she slid in beside me on the couch. With her head resting on my shoulder and her hand over my heart, I fell asleep.

Blissful.

Sated.

And free.

EPILOGUE

SLOANE

TWO MONTHS LATER...

I LET OUT A BREATH, HOPING TO DISPEL THE nervous energy that went along with it, but it was no use. It was with me for the long haul. Grayson settled his large, warm palm onto my bouncing knee, and I turned to look at him.

"Everything will be fine."

Biting my lip, I nodded. That was easy for him to say. He wasn't the one returning to the States—returning to a mother he didn't even know—after being abducted and MIA for three months.

The plane jolted as the landing gears were deployed, the mechanical whirring sound filling the cabin. Around us, hundreds of people began to shift in their seats, the excitement of being in a completely new country amplifying.

Grayson squeezed my thigh again, and I stared down at

the Celtic tattoo on the back of his hand. My eyes skated over to the solid gold wedding band now on his ring finger—the one that matched my own.

We'd gotten married as soon as Grayson was well enough, and even though my mother didn't know, I couldn't help but hear her asking me whether I'd rushed into things. I hadn't. I was so confident in Grayson and my relationship that even if my mom disagreed, I didn't care. I found the person I wanted to be with. My growling, possessive, protective person. The one I wanted to be with...

Forever.

The voice of the head stewardess filled the cabin, her Irish accent more decipherable now that I'd been listening to the same brogue every day. Whether he was whispering dirty things into my ear as he slid inside me or talking to me as we lay in the bath together—his thick chest propping me up, his voice vibrating through my back—I'd grown to recognize the cadence and rhythm of the language as my home.

Turning my head, I looked out the window to see the ground coming up to meet us. As soon as those wheels touched down, I'd be back in America. A moment later, the wheels let out a high-pitched squeal as they made contact, bouncing once before gravity clung to the rubber.

The energy in the cabin turned frenetic, and I couldn't help but feel a little swept up in it all. I watched the seatbelt sign like a hawk, waiting for the light to dim. When it finally did, people were out of their seats, kids squawking about wanting to go home, go to the hotel, or go to the beach.

When Grayson stood to get our carry-on luggage, people

stepped back to give him the space he needed. Yes, we'd flown in economy for this leg to LA, but it had seemed so... normal. I'd grown up with wealth, but with Grayson's downgrade to sentinel, it had meant a cut in what he earned, too.

Did I begrudge him for it? Never, because it meant the man I loved would survive.

Plus, he was still the biggest bad-ass around.

He got our luggage down, as well as the luggage for an elderly couple that had been sitting behind us. The trio slipped into Gaelic as we waited, and I listened with a smile on my face. I'd started to learn some words and phrases, although most of them were related to sex at this point, but I did pick up Grayson telling them to enjoy their fiftieth wedding anniversary.

He said he hoped he looked as in love when we reached our fiftieth.

I could hardly believe that less than twenty-four hours ago, Grayson and I had gotten married in a small church with only two witnesses. Fallon, of course, and Caolan, the clan's Master. The service was quick but filled with no less love than the grand wedding my father would've insisted upon.

Grayson held out his hand to me, and I blinked up into his face. "We're moving, lass."

I looked around. Sure enough, the people that had been sitting in front of us were all gone. Leaping from my seat, I walked out onto the aerobridge, then into the terminal. I hadn't told anyone where we were going on our honeymoon—not even my mom, who I'd gotten in contact with via the club Dagger worked at while Grayson was recovering. She'd been worried sick, but after I told her I was safe and well, it seemed to placate her.

My new husband entwined his fingers with mine as we walked through the mass of people. I could feel everyone's eyes on Grayson. Some wary. Some curious. Some threatened. He either didn't notice or didn't give a shit. I was betting it was the latter.

We were almost through the terminal when I drew to an abrupt stop.

"Sloane?" Grayson asked, looking around, trying to find the threat.

But there was none.

My heart was tap dancing with my ribcage as I moved my head to get a better look at a woman waiting just ahead—a woman with the same color hair as mine. She had come, but how did she know we'd be here?

When my mom's clear gray eyes locked on mine, it didn't matter how. Grayson released my hand, and I ran to her. Chantelle wrapped me in her arms tightly, the smell of salt tears coming soon after.

"I thought I'd never see you again," she said against my shoulder, her words muffled.

"Me, too," I replied.

When she pulled back, she took me by the shoulders and looked at me. *Marveled* at me.

"How long do you have?"

"I had to travel in on a fake passport, so maybe a month? Aidan has men everywhere."

She nodded. "I'll take a month." Her eyes flickered over

my shoulder, and she released me. I spun around to face my mom and my husband. The look she gave him was her 'cop' look, I had no doubt.

"Mom, you remember Grayson, right?"

"Yeah, I do," she replied, her voice tight. "He stole you right out from under our noses. What is he doing here?"

Backtracking, I took him by the hand and showed her our rings.

Her eyes widened.

"We got married," I said softly, hoping she was okay with this. Needing her to be okay with this. I hadn't had my mother in my life for eighteen years, so there was some serious ground to make up.

Gray eyes glittering, she looked back at me. "Did he force you? Coerce you? I know what men like him are like."

"Men like what?" a dark voice drawled.

Chantelle turned. "Dagger, thank God you're here. Sloane says she's married to..." she jabbed a thumb at Grayson, "... this thug."

Dagger's green eyes narrowed to slits on Grayson's face, but Grayson stayed relaxed. He knew how to play this game. "You're the motherfucker who stole our Sloane. What the fuck do you think you're doing?"

Our Sloane?

"The same thing you did with Chantelle," he replied easily. "Claiming the woman I love as my own."

The pair stared at each other for a long moment before Dagger put out his hand to shake. Grayson took it, the men sizing each other up before finally releasing their holds.

Placing a possessive hand on the small of my mother's

back, he led the way out to baggage claim, leaving Grayson and me to follow.

"Well, that went well," I said.

"Aye, it did." He smiled, placing a hand on my belly. "Now, let's see how they take the other news."

ANOTHER EPILOGUE

ORIN

FUCK, I WAS IN TROUBLE. RUNNING MY HAND under the flap of my jacket and over the left side of my ribs, I pulled it out and swore out loud this time at the amount of blood that was staining my fingers. Jesus, *fuck,* whatever internal organ had been hit, it was bleeding like a motherfucker.

Just another scar to add to the collection, I thought darkly.

I yanked on the wheel to go around a red tractor trailer, which was in the wrong fucking lane on the motorway, speeding past him while my vision turned blurry. I was only a few miles from Galway, but it might as well be a thousand. I could feel my head becoming lighter and lighter with each pint of blood I lost.

Wiping the sweat from my forehead, I concentrated on getting home—or at least getting close to another clan member's house. If I passed out on the side of the road now, there was a good chance I would end up in the hospital, and if I ended up in the hospital, there was a good chance I would end up in jail. They wouldn't be able to prove any of the murders I've committed over the years in the clan's interests, but I was sure they'd find something to pin on me.

The headlights swept over a sign for Galway, and I yanked on the wheel, blinking rapidly to try and clear my vision.

Not much farther.

Not much farther.

Rain started to patter down on the windshield—softly at first—before the droplets became huge, tapping against the glass like they were demanding entry into the car. The Rover's wipers sprung into action, wiping away the water, but the moment seemed to smear my thoughts. Where the hell was I going, and why were my ribs hurting?

Reaching down, I touched them, clenching my teeth when pain harpooned through me. My fingers were red. *Blood.* What the hell...

Then I remembered. The shoot-out with the Bèar clan's Reaper—Brian Farrell. Ever since Sloane's abduction, Finnan and Mannix King had been fighting among themselves—tit-for-tat acts of revenge. The hijackings had stopped, but there had been plenty more dissent among the two clans.

Tonight, Finnan had sent me into the Bèar clan's territory to take out an important ally in their business dealings—a cop with enough clout to order his men to look the other way when Mannix had business that needed to be done. The hit had been successful, but that bastard Farrell had been lying in wait for me.

The shot he'd gotten off was the one I was currently bleeding out from—the one I would die from *if* I didn't get some medical help.

I was in the outer suburbs now, the streets familiar. I was close to Kent's place. Given the bastard had stolen Finnan's woman away from him, he was a fucking clan pariah at this point, but he was still clan.

The Rover bumped up over the gutter as I pulled in and undid my seatbelt, the wipers increasing their side-to-side action with the swelling rain. Sliding from the driver's seat, I lost my footing and landed hard on the asphalt. With more effort than I thought would be necessary, I clutched at the driver's side handle and hauled myself level once more.

Weaving unsteadily on my feet, I made it to the front door and pounded once before slipping, losing my balance, and collapsing onto the hard concrete step. The rain slapped at me. I closed my eyes, breathing out of my mouth. The night was ripped away when a shaft of light landed on my face, then got bigger. I was too tired to open my eyes, but I managed to breathe out the word "help" before I was swept away in a kaleidoscope of blood.

Of pain.

Of nothingness.

THE
WARLORD

USA TODAY BESTSELLING AUTHOR
KALLY ASH

Made in the USA
Middletown, DE
29 June 2024